As if sensing her need, Paige leaned forward and gently kissed her. Amalia took her head in her hands and held her for a longer kiss. Their tongues met. The sensation almost made Amalia cry out. When Paige grabbed her arms and held her tightly, she welcomed the pain. It meant she was coming alive again. She could feel need and want and desire. And right now she desired this woman like no other.

Paige pushed her down against the hard rock. It bit into her back, but she didn't care. Paige's mouth was firm and insistent. Her tongue thrust deeply, eliciting a moan from Amalia. Her touch burned a path along Amalia's arms and breasts and thighs. She silently cursed the jeans she wore, wanting to feel Paige's fingers against her bare flesh. Almost frantically, she ran her hands along Paige's muscular arms, firm chest, and taut stomach. Her skin felt on fire. She pulled her own T-shirt off, urging Paige's mouth to her breasts. Paige suckled her nipples through the bra and then pulled it aside to take them one by one into her mouth.

"Oh, God, Paige! I want you to make love to me." The plea came unbidden to her lips.

LOOKING FOR NAIAD?

**Buy our books at
www.naiadpress.com**

**or call our toll-free number
1-800-533-1973**

**or by fax (24 hours a day)
1-850-539-9731**

Strangers in the Night

BARBARA JOHNSON

THE NAIAD PRESS, INC.
1999

Printed in the United States of America on acid-free paper
First Edition

Editor: Christine Cassidy
Cover designer: Bonnie Liss (Phoenix Graphics)
Typesetter: Sandi Stancil

Library of Congress Cataloging-in-Publication Data

Johnson, Barbara, 1955–
    Strangers in the night / Barbara Johnson.
        p.   cm.
    ISBN 1-56280-256-9   (alk. paper)
    I. Title.
PS3560.037174S77   1999
813'.54—dc21   98-48232
                                                                      CIP

I dedicate this novel to a loyal Canadian reader,
Sue Crysler,
who passed away in March 1999,
and to all those left behind
when a loved one is taken too soon.

Acknowledgments

A big thanks to Collin Neal for his help with Hawaiian facts, Skip Burns for his friendship and snorkeling lessons, hosts Brent and Scot of Hale Kipa 'O Pele for their gracious hospitality, and Dr. Scott Mann for his medical expertise.

To Kathleen and Therese, a special thank-you for keeping me sane and laughing. You are two terrific women.

And to the Naiad folks — Christi and Bonnie and Sandi and, of course, Barbara and Donna and all the others — I love you gals!

As always, I also thank the following bookstores for hosting book signings for *Bad Moon Rising*: HerStory Bookstore (Hellam, PA), Lambda Rising (DC and Rehoboth Beach, DE), Lammas Women's Books and More (DC), and Phoenix Rising (Richmond, VA). As more and more gay and lesbian bookstores vanish from our community, the survivors deserve even more our support. And I'm sorry to report that HerStory has indeed become another casualty. Thank you, Kathy, for seven wonderful years.

About the Author

Barbara Johnson wrote the successful *The Beach Affair* and *Bad Moon Rising*, a mystery series featuring lesbian insurance investigator Colleen Fitzgerald. She's also the author of the Regency romance *Stonehurst* and has short stories in six Naiad anthologies: *The Mysterious Naiad, The First Time Ever, Dancing in the Dark, Lady Be Good, The Touch of Your Hand*, and *The Very Thought of You*. She is currently working on the third Colleen Fitzgerald mystery, *Sanctuary*.

Chapter One

The ringing doorbell roused Amalia from her doze on the couch. She sat unmoving, waiting for Sheba to start barking, but then remembered her beloved golden retriever would never bark again. The cancer that had eaten away at Sheba for a year had finally claimed her life. With a deep sigh, Amalia pushed up from the couch and went to the door. She couldn't help but smile when she saw the delivery man loaded down with boxes and bags from Macy's. Her new vacation wardrobe had arrived.

She had the man set the parcels down in the bare

dining room and quickly paid him a tip. She felt like a schoolgirl again as she sat on the polished hardwood floor and unpacked box after box, delighting in the rustle of tissue paper and flash of brightly colored resortwear. She could almost forget the pain and heartache of the past two years — almost, but not quite. It lingered along the edges of her consciousness, ready to creep out like the imaginary monsters under the beds of her childhood. But she had taken one of the many steps toward a full recovery, toward a new life, a life without Kathy.

Amalia left the clothes scattered across the floor and scampered up the stairs, carrying the new swimwear. She paused briefly outside one closed door, feeling the pain grab at her, but she shook her head and entered her bedroom instead. Quickly stripping off her jeans and polo shirt, she slipped into the flower-patterned bikini first. She felt her breath heavy in her chest and had to take two great gulps of air before she could turn to face the full-length mirror propped against one newly painted wall.

She didn't realize she had her eyes closed until the darkness behind her eyelids turned blood red. She opened them slowly and gazed at the figure reflected before her. She was still thin, but she no longer looked like some emaciated fashion model. She was eating right again, and the physical therapy and exercise had finally paid off. She actually had some shape to her body. The doctors had done a good job of putting together her shattered bones. Her legs were long and lean and would become more muscular as her strength and stamina increased enough to let her once again run for miles through the countryside. She was beginning to feel like a woman again. The doctors had not lied to her; the scars that crisscrossed her body were barely noticeable, except for one.

She ran her fingernails along the vertical scar that started above her left breast right at the bra line and continued down her belly to disappear into the bikini bottom. The scar was pink now, like summer's first blush rose. She could still recall the first time she'd seen the mark of the incision — an angry, mottled, crimson welt that split her body in two and seemed to pulse with a life of its own. She'd buried her face into her mother's comforting bosom and sobbed until she had no tears left. She traced it almost lovingly now, feeling the slight ridge in its center. She viewed it as a battle scar, proof of her endurance and strength.

She cocked her head to one side, feeling the silken strands of strawberry-blonde hair move across her shoulders, soft, like a lover's touch. She decided the scar was still too noticeable and stripped off the bikini to put on the blue-and-gold one-piece. She nodded; this one was much better. She next tied a matching blue sarong around her waist. Rising up on her toes, Amalia danced to the tune in her head. The light cotton sarong fluttered against her legs, tickling. After a few minutes, she stopped and laughed out loud. It felt good to laugh again.

The creaking of the old house caught her attention. "Settling noises," Kathy had always said, ever the practical one. Amalia's more fanciful nature, and her Irish grandmother's influence, made them into leprechauns scampering through the air ducts. Well, this time she heard only an old house creaking. She sat on the bed and looked around the room. What now served as her bedroom was to have been the guest room. It was very pretty, with pale lavender

3

walls and matching carpet. The big bay window let in sunshine and fresh air, the sheer lavender curtains billowing slightly in the breeze. The window seat held white cushions adorned with tiny lavender flowers. It had been Kathy and Amalia's intention to match the bedspread and draperies to those cushions, but only the cushions had been done before the accident. And Amalia had forgotten where to find the material.

She lay back on the bed, suddenly exhausted. She was proud of the work she'd done over these last few months, but no one really knew how it nearly drained what life was left in her. After she'd gotten out of the rehabilitation hospital, her friends had convinced her that finishing the renovation of the old stone farmhouse would be the best therapy for her shredded emotions and shattered dreams. In a way, her friends had been right. Part of healing and accepting Kathy's death was to transform the neglected structure into the beautiful showcase it could be, to make their dream come true. They'd scrimped and saved every penny, each taking two jobs. How ironic that money from the accident settlement was what paid for the renovation. Finishing the house was Amalia's final tribute to Kathy and the love they'd shared, and now it was time to let it go.

Most of the furniture was gone. She only had the few pieces necessary to be comfortable, but tomorrow the movers would come and take it to storage. The house was rewired, repaired, and repainted. New copper plumbing ran throughout, and the hardwood floors had been refinished to their original sheen. New windows, new carpeting in the upstairs bedrooms, new bathrooms. New owners.

Amalia suddenly beat her fists against the bed in

frustration and rage. "Damn you, Kathy," she screamed, "why did you have to die?"

She turned and wept into her pillow. She'd thought she had no tears left, but still they came, day after day, night after night. The aches in her body reminded her daily of her ordeal, of her loss. She fought hard against the memories, the anguish. Her lesbian psychiatrist kept telling her she was making good progress. It made Amalia laugh. Today, she had thrown away the doctor's business card and the pills. One more step toward becoming a whole person again.

Amalia didn't know when she stopped crying or when she'd fallen asleep, but the shrill ring of the phone jolted her awake. "Hello?" she mumbled.

"Amalia, darling," Alexander said, "you must be so psyched up."

She smiled at his choice of words. "Actually, I was sleeping in my new bathing suit. Practicing for those lazy days on the beach."

"You can't fool me. I know you've been soaking your pillow again. I hear it in your voice. Do you need me to come over?"

She sat up. "That's okay. I'll be seeing you later tonight, at dinner."

"But I'll have to share you with all those dykes. And then you'll be off to Hawaii for God knows how long." He clicked his tongue. "Really, how many people go to Hawaii with a one-way ticket?"

She chuckled. "You know why I have to go, Alex."

"Yes, I do. And you know I only like to tease you. It's good to hear you laugh. I'm just jealous. All those gorgeous Hawaiian boys over there, and me stuck here. Well, you'll have to squeeze one into your luggage when you come back."

"You can count on it."

"See you tonight, sweetheart."

Amalia hung up the phone and got out of bed. She would miss Alexander terribly. He seemed to be the only person in her world right now who didn't treat her like some fragile doll. Everyone still tiptoed around her, afraid to even mention Kathy's name. But they all jabbered incessantly about Sheba, as if the death of a pet was somehow a more acceptable topic of conversation. Even her parents couldn't seem to grasp that the dog's death had reached deep inside her and wrenched her heart out. But Sheba and the house had been the last physical reminders of Kathy, and tomorrow it would be over once and for all.

She took off the bathing suit and put her jeans and shirt back on. She had to pack the clothes that had come from Macy's. It took more than one trip, but she finally had everything piled on the bed. She put a CD of Hawaiian music in the stereo to get her in the mood. She couldn't help but sway to the music, which convinced her that she'd sign up for hula lessons once she got settled on the island. Finally, everything was carefully folded or rolled and packed in the suitcases. She decided she'd wear her jeans on the plane, but she chose a new Hawaiian print shirt and the sparkling white Keds to go with them. The only thing left to do in the morning was the carry-on bag.

As she locked the last suitcase, the photo on her bedside table caught her eye. Kathy's brown eyes looked shyly into the camera, her head tilted slightly downward. Her dark blonde hair was parted in the middle, with bangs feathering back from her face. The longest layer brushed gently against the back of her neck. She wore an orange T-shirt with a red bandanna circling her throat. The smile was tentative, yet mischievous.

The day it was taken, they'd gone on a picnic with Alexander and his lover at the time to Lake Linganore up in Frederick County. Alex's lover was studying to be a fashion photographer and had cajoled them all into posing. As usual, Amalia hated the photos of herself, but she'd paid to have the one of Kathy enlarged. She smiled as she thought of Kathy's protests.

"Why do you want to have that on the nightstand?" she'd asked. "I look so dopey."

Amalia kissed her. "No, you look sweet. C'mon, it's a great photo. I think we should put it on our Christmas card."

Kathy vigorously shook her head. "That's where I put my foot down. No tacky photo Christmas cards, especially when it's my photo. Okay, I'll let you have the nightstand, but that's it."

They'd fallen laughing onto the bed and playfully wrestled for the photo. Before long, it had fallen to the floor as their playfulness had turned passionate. Amalia thought Kathy had made love to her that night like no other time. It was as if they were newly together, yet they'd been a couple for four years. Who could have known that a year later, almost to the day, Kathy would be stolen from her in the most horrifying way possible?

Amalia shook her head. She'd promised herself she wouldn't think about the accident. It had actually been several days since she'd last thought about it. Who could blame her now, with Kathy's image caught so vividly in the photo? Amalia went to the nightstand and snatched the photo up. She started to put it in a box destined for storage, but on second thought reopened a suitcase and shoved the photo underneath all the clothes. Kathy had been the most important part of her life, and she couldn't just pretend the past had never happened.

She looked at her watch. Damn! It had gotten so late. She was supposed to meet Alexander and the others at the Niwano Hana Japanese restaurant in Bethesda in twenty minutes. Oh well, she'd be late again. She jumped in the shower and then dressed in black tailored pants and a purple silk blouse. On a whim, she wore her pearl choker and matching earrings. It had been a long time since she'd dressed up for dinner or anything else. May as well make her farewell dinner fashionable as well as memorable. She only hoped she could endure it.

Three hours later, Amalia was ready to bolt. All her friends were being too sweet and so incredibly annoying. She could tell that deciding to abandon her life in Maryland and run off to Hawaii was going to be one of the best decisions she'd ever made. She sighed as Heather ordered yet another round of sake.

"Really, Amalia," Jacquie was saying, "I still don't understand why you're running away like this. You might as well be joining the Peace Corps for all we'll ever see you again."

"I actually did think of joining the Peace Corps, but they said my medical condition would prevent that."

"Medical condition?" Randy chimed in. "What

medical condition? I thought you were all patched up and ready to dance?"

"I guess they thought I might have a heart attack or something."

"But that's ridiculous. The doctors said you're as good as new." Randy looked at Amalia over the top of her glasses. "Didn't they?"

Amalia laughed. "They always say that, but I do have that abdominal aortic aneurysm that needs to be monitored. An ultrasound might not be standard equipment in some Third World countries."

Alexander pursed his lips. "Oh, I just love it when you talk medical. It reminds me that I must find a rich doctor to take care of me."

"So," George cut in, "are you happy with the new owners of the house?"

"They seem nice. The wife loves animals and gardening, and the husband collects toy trains. It doesn't really matter now anyway. They move in tomorrow and I move out. I finished the house like Kathy and I wanted. It's someone else's turn to worry about it."

The table fell silent at the mention of Kathy's name. Amalia wanted to shake them all as they looked everywhere but at her. Only Alexander looked her in the eye and smiled as he patted her hand. "You did a damn fine job too. Kathy would be so proud."

"You know," Amalia said as she sipped her sake, "you don't need to treat me like someone who needs to be protected. I can talk about Kathy without getting hysterical. She's been gone two years, and I've grown a lot in that time. Who would have thought a femme like me could renovate a house?"

9

Jacquie looked sheepish. "We're sorry. It's just hard to deal with it. The terrible accident, Kathy's dying, your ordeal in the hospital all those months . . . We love you."

Amalia searched six earnest faces. "But I've moved beyond all that, don't you see? And all my friends have helped me, even if you do skirt the issues." She reached around the table and touched each one lightly on the hand. "I'm going to miss each and every one of you, but I can't say that I'm ever coming back."

Randy laughed. "Well, just be prepared for the hordes to descend upon you over there in paradise. Staying with you will be a hell of a lot cheaper than a hotel."

"Just which island are you going to?" Heather asked.

"Yeah," Sam echoed, "which one?"

"I thought I'd try them all out at first, but I'm leaning toward the Big Island of Hawaii. It's less populated than the others."

"And what about money?" Randy asked with characteristic bluntness. "I know you got a big settlement from the insurance companies, but you spent a lot of it on the house. You can't have much left."

Amalia swallowed nervously. She hated talking about money. Only Alexander and her parents knew just how much money she had received, and it was enough that she'd never have to work again. Even her medical bills not covered by insurance and the house expenses had barely put a dent in her bank account. She was, literally, a millionaire several times over, but she'd give it all up to have Kathy back.

"Oh, I expect she'll get some fun job over there,"

Alex said, saving her from having to answer. "It's not like she'll need a lot. I mean, no more winter coats and boots, no more snow tires, no more astronomical heating bills."

Amalia smiled her thanks at him and then looked at her watch. "I'm sorry to have to break this up, but I go to settlement at the real estate lawyer's early tomorrow, and then the movers are coming. I have to be out of the house by noon, and my plane for L.A. leaves at three. It's been a wonderful dinner, but I really do have to go." She stood up.

"How are you getting to the airport?" George asked.

"I've called for a limo."

Jacquie raised her eyebrows. "Ooohhh, a limo. We're going out in style, aren't we?" She got up and kissed Amalia's cheek. "Not that you don't deserve it."

"What'd you do with your car?" Sam interjected.

"I donated it to the Salvation Army. They're coming by tomorrow to pick it up."

They all stood then and clustered around Amalia, each one wanting to get in one more hug, one more kiss. She felt the tears well up in her eyes. She tried to speak, but the words stuck in her throat. Alexander gently took her arm. "Let's go, sweetheart," he said and led her out of the restaurant. She looked back once more and saw five serious faces. She could tell that Heather and Jacquie were crying, and maybe even George and Sam too. Randy, ever the stoic butch, put an arm around her weeping lover. She would shed no tears, that one. At least, not in public. With a final wave, Amalia left the restaurant.

* * * * *

11

She woke early the next morning. The sunlight barely peeped around the edges of the window shades. She lay in the big bed and listened one more time to the house. It was very quiet, an almost deathlike stillness. Even the creaks were silent. There was no click of Sheba's claws on the hardwood floors of the hallway, no labored breathing at the foot of her bed.

In her mind's eye, Kathy came to life, stooping down to hug an ecstatic Sheba who no longer limped in pain but leapt with the energy of a puppy. And Kathy's mangled body was whole again, her brown eyes sparkling with laughter and love. Amalia smiled as she opened her eyes and got out of bed. Pain is only for the living, she thought as she washed up and packed the last of her things.

But a new life awaited her in a tropical paradise, one in which she knew Kathy and Sheba would always be with her, in her heart.

Chapter Two

Paige threw her book across the room in frustration. These damn final exams were going to drive her crazy. Thank God her two years of torture were almost over. No, make that six years. You had to count the four undergraduate years, even if she had partied her way through them. She was tempted to go out to the Lemon Tree bar tonight, but she knew an evening of drinking and flirting would not give her a clear head for tomorrow's exam in marine mammal physiology. She'd passed her orals with flying colors; her thesis on the homosexual behavior of squids had been quite a hit. It was just this one last exam she had to get through. And Dr. Dalkind was her most onerous professor. His exam would be a bear, and she was convinced he didn't like her. She laughed. It was probably because she got more women than he ever did.

She got up from her desk and starting pacing the room, stretching her arms and rolling her shoulders as she walked. She was really feeling restless tonight, almost uneasy. It was rare for her to have a case of pre-exam jitters, but that was the only thing she could attribute it to. The intense course of study this last semester had wiped her out more than she realized. After a few minutes, she stopped pacing, turned on the local progressive rock radio station, and picked up a pair of dumbbells. She worked her biceps until they hurt, then switched to her triceps. Sometimes a fierce pain could distract her thoughts, but tonight it wasn't working.

She threw the dumbbells down. They landed with a satisfying thud. She hoped her obnoxious neighbor down below was home. He could be such an asshole — playing his radio or television until all hours of the night, taking such long showers that he used up all the hot water before she could take hers. She couldn't move out soon enough.

Speaking of moving . . . She got a shoebox out of her closet and started rifling through its contents. It held dozens of university brochures and numerous letters in answer to her own queries. She had decided to take a year off before continuing with her Ph.D., but she still had to apply and be accepted somewhere. She was confident that she'd be accepted wherever she applied. After all, she'd maintained a 4.0 every year and would be graduating at the top of her class. If old Dr. Dalkind didn't screw her over, that is. Several universities had even recruited her, but so far they all left her cold.

She looked through the brochures again and reread the letters. She put the "definitely nots" in one pile and the "maybes" in another. Then she eliminated others by geographic location. She'd had enough of harsh winters, having spent the last two in Massachusetts and the previous four in Alaska. That left schools down South or out West. Despite the numerous choices in places like Florida, South Carolina, and Alabama, she decided the South was too redneck and racist for her taste, which left the West. Yes, she could handle Texas or California or even Oregon. Hell, maybe she *would* go to Texas and become a cowboy.

The thought made her smile. She could still remember the cowboy outfit she'd had as a young tomboy. She'd worn that thing until it literally fell apart. Her mom had hoped she'd switch to more appropriate feminine attire, but Paige had coerced her unmarried aunt into taking her shopping for new cowboy duds. Aunt Maggie had even sprung for real cowboy boots, not the fake kiddie kind. God, she hadn't seen Aunt Maggie in almost eleven years. She remembered how scandalized everyone had been when her aunt had left town with that "truck-drivin' woman." Boy, was Paige glad when it was her turn to leave that narrow-minded small town in Iowa. On impulse, she got the phone and dialed home.

"Hey, Ma, how's it going?" she asked when she

heard the chirpy voice of her mother. "Haven't talked to you in a bit. Thought I'd call and catch up."

"It's been almost a month," her mom scolded. "I know you're studying for finals, but surely your family deserves to hear from you?"

Paige was tempted to point out that the phone worked both ways, but she said instead, "Well, my last exam is tomorrow and then I'm a free woman."

"Are you coming home?" Her mom's voice rose a notch when she got excited. "Your dad will be glad to have you around. He's got lots of projects around the house you can help him with."

I'd rather stick a fork in my eye, Paige thought. "I won't be able to stay long. I have a job lined up." The lie rolled glibly off her tongue.

"Where?"

"Montana."

"What kind of place is Montana for a marine biologist? They don't have any oceans there."

"I'm doing a stint with a paleontologist. Marine fossils."

Before Paige could say any more, her mom began reciting all the local gossip — who was getting married and who had died. She mentioned that an old class-mate of Paige's had been arrested for dealing drugs.

When she finally stopped to take a breath, Paige asked, "Say, Ma, do you ever hear from Aunt Maggie?"

There was a long pause. Paige could almost hear her mom thinking.

"I don't think we've heard from her in, gosh, more than six years. I believe the last Christmas card we got came from Ohio or Kansas or someplace like that. I'll have to ask your Uncle Calvin if he knows. What-ever made you think of her?"

Paige laughed. "Just cowboys, Ma. Just cowboys. Well, gotta go. One more night of studying. Give my love to Dad."

She hung up the phone before her mother could complain. She only felt a little guilty lying about having a job in Montana. Spending the summer in corn country helping her dad renovate their house was the last thing she wanted to do. The trouble was, she didn't know what she *did* want.

She flopped on the bed and put her hands behind her head. She seemed to notice for the first time the cracks in the ceiling, which made her sit up and look around the small studio apartment that had been home for two years. The walls were badly in need of a paint job; the faded blue carpeting was pretty threadbare. The kitchen appliances were avocado-colored, a sure sign they were at least twenty-five years old. The place came furnished with functional yet ugly furniture. The women she'd brought home weren't impressed with the place. Still, it was clean and affordable on a graduate student's salary. She'd always managed to find jobs here and there on campus, helping out in different departments. She'd even tried teaching a biology lab. The trouble was, nothing ever kept her interest for long. That was one reason why she'd decided to go for a master's and then a Ph.D. She wouldn't have to look for a full-time job if she was still a student.

She got out of bed and picked up the book she'd thrown across the room. When she opened it to a full-color rendering of the innards of a California sea lion, she decided to order pizza and a six-pack of Coke. It was going to be a long night.

* * * * *

A week later, Paige eagerly scanned the bulletin board where Dr. Dalkind liked to post grades. She traced with her finger down the list looking for her name.

"Yesssss!" she shouted and jumped for joy. The old coot had given her an *A*. With her grade-point average intact, she could practically write her own ticket to the next university. That reminded her to check her mail. She was surprised to see a letter with a Honolulu postmark. She ripped open the envelope. The University of Hawaii was inviting her to pursue her Ph.D. with them. It seemed that one of her professors had contacted them about her, and they were eager for bright young students to join their doctoral program. Paige couldn't imagine anyone not wanting to go to school in Hawaii. Hell, she'd go check it out just for the vacation. Now she really had something to tell her mother, and it wouldn't be a lie. But first, she had to tell Marianne.

She made her way to Barnaby Hall, the undergraduate dorm where her latest girlfriend was staying. Marianne would be leaving in two days to go home to Maine for the summer, and Paige figured that would be the end of their relationship. They'd both known it was nothing permanent, but it sure had been nice to have someone these last six months or so. Marianne would be returning to Dartmouth in the fall for her senior year. Paige took the stairs two at a time and sprinted down the hallway. She rapped on the door.

"Hey, Marianne, it's me! I've got great news."

Muffled sounds came through the door. Paige knocked again. "Marianne?"

Suddenly the door was flung open. Marianne stood in the doorway, a towel wrapped around her short, curvy body. Her dark curls were tousled, and her face was flushed. She couldn't quite meet Paige's eyes. "Now's not a good time," she whispered as she leaned forward. The towel dropped a bit, giving Paige an enticing view of creamy breasts and cleavage. Paige couldn't help the jolt of wanting that flashed through her.

She kissed Marianne's lips and then gave them a light nip. "If you're just getting ready to take a shower," she murmured, "I'll join you."

Marianne pushed her away. "You don't understand . . ."

"Who is it, baby?" a voice called out from the room. A male voice.

Paige looked at Marianne, who looked like she was going to throw up. Before Marianne could stop her, she pushed her way into the room. There, on the bed where she and Marianne had spent numerous hours making passionate love, sat a man she'd never seen before. He was stark raving naked. On the bed beside him was the dildo she had bought for Marianne on a whim. They'd never used it. "Too penislike," Marianne had complained.

"Who the hell are you?" Paige barked.

"Who the hell are you?" he shot back.

Marianne stood between them. Her face had blanched pure white, and her black eyes darted back and forth like they always did when she was nervous.

She held out her hands to Paige. "I can explain all this . . ."

"What's to explain?" Paige snarled. "You've been fucking a man behind my back! How long has this been going on?"

The man looked at Marianne and then pointed at Paige. "You've been sleeping with her?"

"Please, Richard, it was just a lark. I wanted to experiment a little. That's all."

Paige felt the blood rush to her cheeks. "An experiment? That's all I was to you these last six months? An experiment? I hope the hell you two have been using condoms."

Richard stood up and approached her, but she was gratified to see she was taller than he was. That, plus the fact that he was buck naked, must have made him realize he was at a disadvantage, and he backed off again and sat on the bed. He pulled the sheet over himself. "Maybe I'm the one who should be asking if *you* used condoms?"

Marianne touched Paige's arm. "Can we talk about this later, please?"

Paige looked at her. "No, we can't. I came to tell you that I am leaving for Hawaii tomorrow. See you around."

With that, she turned on her heel and stalked out the door. She was fuming, and she didn't really know if she was angry because Marianne had been screwing a man all this time or if it was because her ego was bruised. She'd never had a woman leave her for a man before — not that she knew of anyway. As she strode rapidly across campus, she felt her anger draining away. Well, she had been coming to say good-bye, more or less. This way, there'd be no tears and no regrets. At least, not on her part.

She wasn't really leaving for Hawaii tomorrow, but that scene in Marianne's room had made up her mind. She'd leave as soon as she could get her stuff packed up and shipped out. She still had the rest of this month plus one more paid on her apartment, but she didn't care. She'd see if her friend Rory wanted to move in for the time. He always lived hand-to-mouth anyway.

The next few days were a whirlwind of activity. Her first priority, after phoning the university with her acceptance, was to visit a travel agent to book the cheapest flight possible. For the move, she only packed the things she really cared about, like her books, and had them shipped home. Her parents weren't happy when she told them she wouldn't make it to Iowa for the summer at all. They were even more unhappy when she withdrew the little bit of money she'd inherited from her grandmother and told them she was going to Hawaii with it. Her mom always thought she'd save it for when she got married. It always made Paige laugh when her mom brought up the subject of marriage, as if she didn't already know Paige's proclivities.

She told her landlord that she was leaving for a few weeks and was having someone housesit for her. She'd write him from Hawaii next month and let him know she wouldn't be back. That was one reason why she'd insisted on a month-to-month lease. Rory had been ecstatic when she offered him the apartment.

He'd overstayed his welcome where he lived now, and this would give him until the end of June to find a new place. He came over for dinner on her last night.

"Rory," she said as they sat on the porch with their after-dinner cognacs, "I don't understand why you can't get a steady job and find a place of your own. You must get awfully tired always being a guest, and an unwanted one at that."

"You know I don't have the stamina for a full-time job, and I'd lose my disability checks. Besides, this is too much fun. It's like traveling around Europe on the Eurailpass."

Paige frowned. "I don't see the correlation."

"I get to see different places cheaply. My disability checks are just enough to make me welcome for a while. I do pay for my own groceries."

"Maybe you should think about moving into one of those houses. You know, like Waddell House over on Sixty-fourth."

He rolled his eyes. "I may not be able to work, dear, but I am not an invalid. I'll go there when I'm ready to die."

She bit her lip in frustration. Rory was HIV positive, and she worried about him. It had taken her a long time to get him to apply for disability, but he rarely used the other services open to him. He occasionally would visit the clinic, but even then he had to be really sick. Fortunately, those times had been few so far. She wondered what would happen to him once she left.

She tried one more time. "Waddell House is not a hospice. It's not for people who are dying."

"Paige, darling, I know you mean well, but those

houses *are* for people who are dying. Is there a cure for this disease yet?"

She was annoyed to feel anger. "Don't play this semantics game with me, Rory. You know what I mean."

He patted her on the knee. She noticed how transparent his skin looked; she could see the fine blue veins. "Don't you worry that little head of yours. I just want you to go to Hawaii and find some gorgeous young thing to sweep you off your feet."

She grinned. "Don't you mean one that I'll sweep off her feet?"

He put his hand to his breast. "Pardon me. I did not mean to offend your butch sensibilities."

She impulsively leaned over and gave him a big hug. "I'm going to miss you so much."

"Me too," he said quietly.

They both stopped speaking and just let the chill night air stir over them. She huddled deeper into her jacket. For a moment it seemed like even the traffic noise had died. She heard birds chirping softly, settling down for the night. Even the more raucous starlings were silent. A light breeze rustled the leaves on the trees. Paige actually began to feel a tad nostalgic for the university town that she'd called home for two years. It was a feeling almost foreign to her. She looked over at Rory, liking the way a shock of black hair fell over his forehead. She had surprised herself, liking a man so much, even a gay one. Previously, she'd had no use for any of them, but somehow Rory had gained her trust and her friendship. He'd been her best friend for almost two years, helping her through rough times with studies and with women.

And he was the one who theorized that her commitment phobia and mistrust stemmed from a disastrous relationship with an older woman. She tried to help him too, when he'd let her.

"Remember when you asked me to think about having a kid with you?" she asked.

He laughed. "I'll never forget the shocked look on your face." He punched her arm lightly. "You thought I was joking."

"Well, I don't exactly look like the mother type."

"You have all the right equipment." He closed his eyes and leaned against a post. "But it doesn't matter now, does it? I guess it's good I found out before I talked you into it."

"Yeah."

He stood up and stretched. "Well, guess I'll go to bed now. I'm a bit tired."

She stood and gave him a big squeezing hug. He was staying with her the last night in the apartment, but they'd agreed he'd leave early in the morning so there'd be no awkward good-byes. He liked to spend his days at the local gay community center. This was, in effect, their good-bye.

"You take care of yourself," she said.

"You too."

She watched him go inside and felt the suspicious prickling of tears in her eyes. She dashed them away. She couldn't remember the last time she'd cried, and she wasn't about to start now.

The next morning, Paige wrote a quick good-bye note to Rory and left her car keys. She'd signed over the title of her old VW to him for one dollar. A friend drove her to the bus station where she boarded a bus for Boston, the location of the closest airport. She'd managed to get all her clothes into just one suitcase by eliminating anything remotely meant for cold weather. Her only nod to the cold was the jacket she wore. She figured if she needed anything else, she could buy it in Hawaii.

The bus headed out of town, past the university, past Barnaby Hall, and past the Lemon Tree bar where she'd spent many a weekend night playing pool and playing women. If the truth were known, she was happier to be leaving than she let on.

Chapter Three

It was a sunny Thursday afternoon when Amalia's plane landed at Honolulu Airport on the island of Oahu. She'd spent four days in L.A., and the time difference from the West Coast gained her two hours. She hadn't made reservations at a hotel in Honolulu, deciding to take her chances once she got there. She had also decided against a rental car because she'd only be on the island a few days. She asked the cab driver to recommend a hotel, and he told her about one of the only Hawaiian-owned motels on the chain of islands.

"The family who owns this motel are native Hawaiians," he explained, seemingly pleased when she agreed to stay there. "Most of the others are owned by big Japanese conglomerates."

"Do they have just one motel?" she asked.

"Oh no," he said as he drove from the airport. "They also have one in Hilo on the Big Island and one on Maui. You'll find them all very pleasant and immaculate. Will you be visiting the other islands?"

Amalia leaned back against the seat, glad for the air conditioning. "I hope to. I definitely want to go to the Big Island. I might settle permanently there."

He grinned. "Another *haole* taken by the idea of living in paradise. It is wonderful here, but expensive. And work is hard to find."

She didn't answer, but looked with dismay out the window at the passing scenery. Honolulu was a busy city, dirty and noisy like any other. It didn't seem very paradiselike. It had the same strip malls, the same automobile dealers, the same fast-food joints, the same chains of hotels and motels, and the same hordes of people as other cities. Cars, traffic, noise, rampant development, and pollution — that was the legacy the white explorers and missionaries had brought to Hawaii. Just as she was beginning to think she'd made a mistake in coming, the cab rounded a corner and she saw the sparkling blue waters of the Pacific Ocean. The beach was crowded with people.

"We're in Waikiki now," the driver said. "That's the famous beach over there."

She looked to her left. "Could they get the buildings any closer?" she commented. The only thing that separated the sand from the hotels and stores was the wide avenue on which they drove.

27

He laughed without humor. "Don't worry, the whole island isn't like this. And the others are very different."

As he continued driving, large shade trees took the place of tall buildings, and green space replaced shopping malls. Amalia couldn't help but gasp as the unmistakable profile of Diamond Head loomed before them. The extinct volcano rose majestically above the tops of trees, a reminder of the island's primordial glory. It seemed so incongruous to see this magnificent piece of nature in the midst of all this man-made chaos, almost like a conquered beast on display.

"Glorious, isn't it?" the driver said, pride obvious in his voice.

"Yes. Can you go to the top?"

"Only with a special tour, but it's worth it."

She watched through the back window as the mountain disappeared. They were on the outskirts of the city now. The taxi pulled up in front of a sprawling single-level motel. She paid the driver, and he carried her luggage to the lobby.

"Take good care of my friend here," he said to the young woman behind the counter. He winked at Amalia as he left.

She approached the counter and smiled at the clerk. "I hope you have a room."

She nodded her affirmative and said, "*Aloha.* Welcome to Hawaii." She handed Amalia a form to fill out. After all the paperwork was taken care of, a bellhop took her luggage to the room. She followed him through a maze of corridors and into an atrium open to the outside. The sun streamed in and touched the enormous ferns that grew in abundant profusion in the small space. Amalia stopped a moment to take it all in; she'd never seen ferns so tall and with leaves so big. They walked along another corridor and then passed by a small pool in another sunlit atrium. Two children splashed in the pale blue water, while a woman Amalia assumed to be their mother lounged on a wicker chaise and read a book. Just seeing them, she could feel the tension in her muscles relax.

She and the bellhop finally arrived at her room. He opened the door and waved her in. She gave him a tip and turned to survey the room. It was nothing fancy, but it was neat and clean. A single queen-size bed sat in the middle, facing an entertainment console that housed a TV and nothing else. The curtains and bedspread were decorated with a birds-of-paradise print. The light green carpet was obviously new. The white walls were decorated with stunning black and white portraits of various hula dancers, both male and female. Amalia examined one of them more closely.

The woman in the photo was perhaps one of the most exquisite she'd ever seen. Her hair was long and dark. On her head she wore a crown of sharp-tipped triangular leaves that covered her forehead and from under which she gazed seriously into the camera. Her lips were slightly parted, the smile ever so faint. A lei of leaves looped around her neck and then crisscrossed to cover her naked breasts but left her midriff bare. Her arms were down by her sides, the wrists circled with the same leaves as the lei and the wreath on her head. Around her hips she wore a patterned cloth wrap tied low on her belly, exposing her navel. Amalia looked at the signature — Kim Taylor Reece.

"Hmmm," she said, wondering about the sex of the photographer. She made a mental note to ask someone at the motel. From the content of the photos, this photographer no doubt had a studio somewhere in Hawaii.

She looked at her watch and decided to unpack later. She wanted to explore the city, dirty and crowded though it was. The girl at the counter had given her several bus schedules and told her that the bus service in Honolulu and vicinity was one of the best in the United States. Amalia would see just how good it was.

Night had fallen by the time Paige arrived on Oahu. Her travel agent had told her the city bus system was excellent, so she bypassed the rental car counters and instead caught a shared cab from the airport. She needed to save money wherever she could. The city sparkled with light, outshining the stars that glittered high overhead. The hustle and bustle of the people and the traffic made the blood pulse in her veins. She loved the activity, especially after her time in the small university town. The cab dropped her off in front of the Coconut Plaza Hotel in the midst of the city. The gay travel agent she'd consulted had recommended the gay-friendly hotel for someone on a budget. It was also walking distance to just about everything.

The lobby was bright and airy. White wicker furniture with plump cushions invited lounging. Caged birds chirped and sang above the noise of a waterfall fountain. To the right, glass-topped tables and a buffet table indicated where the complimentary breakfast would be served. She plunked her one suitcase down, sauntered over to the counter, and gave her name.

The clerk checked his computer and then smiled at her. "Nonsmoking room, right?" When she nodded, he asked, "Which credit card will you be using?"

"I'd like to pay cash, if that's okay."

"That's fine, but I still need a credit card," he said politely but firmly. "You can pay however you prefer when you check out."

She handed him her American Express card. She used it as little as possible, but knew a credit card was necessary when traveling.

She'd only be on Oahu for four days because she'd decided to stay only long enough to check out the university and a few sights, then she wanted to go on to the Big Island. She wanted to see whales, and she'd heard they were best seen off the Kona coast on the east side. Whales were her favorite marine mammal, but she'd rarely had good luck seeing them on whale-watch cruises she'd taken off the coast of Massachusetts.

She grabbed her bag and took the stairs to her third-floor room. It had a tiny kitchen, two double beds, and the ubiquitous white wicker furniture. A sliding glass door led to a small balcony that overlooked the parking lots of the two buildings behind hers. Well, she mused, she wasn't paying for the view. She went back into the room and unpacked quickly. She was going out on the town. She'd bought a gay travel book that listed all the gay-owned or gay-friendly spots, and she was determined to check out as many of them as possible. Jet lag be damned.

She changed into a black T-shirt and a fresh pair of jeans, both tight and, as a quick glimpse in the mirror confirmed, both showing off her body to its muscular advantage. Her dark blonde hair had gotten a little bit longer than she liked, and she made a mental note to find a salon tomorrow and have it cut. She put on her well-worn Nikes and resolved to find sandals tomorrow too, and a good pair of hiking boots to replace the ones she'd worn out.

Even at this late hour, the streets were alive with people. She was soon overwhelmed by the number of shops selling all sorts of items, from tacky shell-encrusted souvenir ashtrays to expensive and rare black pearls. And everywhere she looked, colorful and splashy Hawaiian shirts and muumuus dominated. All the designers were represented too — Gucci, Versace, Prada, et al. Alongside them stood alley-way malls where locals sold everything from baskets to coral jewelry to fresh leis. On impulse, she bought what the girl told her was a plumeria lei. The scent of the yellow-white blooms was sweet and rich, the very essence of the island. She put it self-consciously around her neck, but liked the contrast of pale flowers against her black shirt. As she walked along Lewers Street down toward Kalakaua Avenue, she saw more people wearing leis and didn't feel so self-conscious anymore. She suddenly realized she was ravenously hungry. She walked into one of the many Japanese noodle houses and ordered a steaming bowl of thick udon noodles with shrimp. The soup was hot and tasty, with tangy traces of horseradish that made her nose run.

With her hunger sated, Paige headed out onto the streets once more. Her travel guide listed a gay bar just around the corner. She smiled when she glimpsed the rainbow flag hanging outside. The bar was mostly filled with men. She ordered a Miller Lite and sat at a patio table that gave her a good view of the street.

Instead of the usual pulsing and loud techno music common in most gay bars, soft Hawaiian instrumentals provided background noise. As she sipped her beer and listened to the music, she could feel her energy draining. She'd been wired a long time, and it was, after all, three in the morning by her body clock.

She watched the people on the street. Honolulu certainly seemed to be quite a melting pot — all races were represented here. After a bit, she could discern the tourists from the locals despite the mostly casual clothing worn by the majority. She felt someone staring at her and looked up to see two women seated at the bar watching her. Dressed in matching sarongs, they were both darkly tanned with long, bleached-blonde hair, whether from the sun or a bottle Paige couldn't rightly tell. Right now, she didn't really care. All she knew was that two gorgeous women who looked like twins in a *Girlfriends* magazine centerfold were smiling at her. She drained her beer and sauntered over to the bar. Two pairs of blue eyes lit up appreciatively.

"Well, hello," she said, lowering her voice to what she'd been told was sexy. "My name's Paige."

The blonde on the right said in a slow Southern accent, "I'm Jennifer, and this is my sister, Judith."

Paige kissed their right hands, noticing that Jennifer wore bright pink polish and Judith wore red. If they got up from their stools, it would be the only way she could tell them apart. "You visiting, or do you live here?" she asked.

"We flew in two days ago, and I must say, you look good enough to eat. What about you, sugar?" Judith's drawl rolled off her tongue.

Paige's jeans suddenly felt too tight and her underwear suspiciously moist. "Just got in tonight," she managed to say with a steady voice. "You two want to spend your time here, or would you like to come to my hotel room? We can raid the minibar." She'd never felt quite so bold before.

Their identical smiles sent shivers up Paige's spine. They slid off their seats simultaneously. Both women were much taller than her, and Paige was no shorty at five-nine. This would be a first, she thought, in more ways than one. If there'd been any lingering memories of Marianne, they were swept away like dust off a porch. She gave a wink to the smirking bartender and led the two women out of the bar and into the street. On the way to the hotel, she stopped where she'd earlier bought her lei and bought one each for Jennifer and Judith. It seemed only fitting that the leis were identical — perfect blue jade blossoms with an intoxicating scent that swirled around them. Paige forgot her exhaustion as she led them up the stairs to her room.

When Paige woke the next morning, it was almost noon and she was alone. The two sisters had left their lingering scents on the sheets and bold red hearts in lipstick on the mirror. She stretched and smiled. Her first night in Hawaii had indeed been paradise — the stuff of romance novels and independent lesbian films. Ever since she'd seen Prince's video *Cream*, Paige had fantasized about having a threesome with twins. She wasn't sure if Jennifer and Judith were twins, but they were close enough. And boy, were they energetic.

Paige had certainly earned her butch credentials last night.

She stretched again and got out of bed. Her arms and shoulders were a bit sore, but pleasantly so — nothing that a hot shower couldn't take care of. She regretted that she hadn't asked the sisters where they were staying, but she knew if she had, she wouldn't accomplish what she came to Hawaii to do. She scrambled into the shower. She had an appointment at the university at one-thirty.

Amalia woke early Saturday morning and took a taxi to the Honolulu Zoo to meet up with a tour group that took people to the summit of Diamond Head. The brochure said the hike lasted three hours, and she hoped she was up to it physically. The day was going to be hot. Amalia was glad she'd thought to buy bottled water. She also packed a light picnic lunch to eat once they got to the top. She wore jeans and a new pair of hiking boots with thick socks. The salesman had assured her she would not get blisters even the first time she wore the boots. Her shirt was a long-sleeved lightweight cotton, and she'd bought a straw hat last night from an old woman who sold goods from a curbside table. She also wore sunglasses and sunblock.

The others in her tour group were mostly Germans and Japanese, and she was certainly the only gay one in the bunch. Everyone was very friendly and, she was glad to notice, most seemed to be as inexperienced a hiker as she.

After ninety minutes, the group finally made it to the top of the extinct volcano. Amalia was exhausted, the uphill walk having sapped what strength she had. Not only had it been grueling physically, but she'd experienced a few episodes of vertigo on the path up the mountain. She was glad they'd be spending a half-hour resting for lunch.

The view was awesome. The jewel-like blue Pacific spread out before her and all around, tiny whitecaps barely visible. Sun diamonds glinted off the surface. Sailboats and what looked like a cruise ship drifted out on the water. Waikiki spread out below on the right, blending into Honolulu. To the left lay the wealthy residential area of Kupikipikio and then Kahala Beach. In the near distance loomed Koko Head, Diamond Head's dormant sister volcano. She took several photos using her new camera with telephoto lens, then gratefully settled onto her blanket for a short lunch.

She shared the blanket with a newlywed American couple and two German couples. The Germans spoke excellent English and spent most of the time exchanging vacation anecdotes with the newlyweds. Amalia smiled and nodded a lot, thankful that they didn't seem to expect her to talk much. She listened keenly when they spoke of sights to see on the Big Island — Waipio Valley, Liliuokalani Gardens, and Kealakekua Bay. The more she heard, the more convinced she was to go directly there after her few days on Oahu. She was eager to find a house and settle into her new life. There would be plenty of time later to go island hopping.

Suddenly, one of the Germans spoke directly to her.

He was the one called Klaus. "You have come here alone?" he asked, his accent barely noticeable.

"Yes, but I'm moving to Hawaii."

The American woman clapped her hands. "How exciting!" She turned to her new husband. "Bob, honey, don't you think you'd like to live here too?"

Bob replied, "In your dreams, Angie. I'm barely able to afford this honeymoon. It's expensive and there are no jobs."

Klaus asked Amalia, "How is it you can move here then?"

His wife, Ingrid, slapped him on the arm. "You do not ask such questions," she chided, her accent much thicker than his. She smiled at Amalia. "My husband is too inquisitive. I apologize for him."

"No need." Amalia smiled back, but she was surprised. She'd always thought Europeans weren't as blunt and nosy as Americans. "I'd like to ask you some questions about the Big Island."

"It is the most amazing place," Klaus volunteered, and the others all nodded in agreement. "You must be sure to go Volcanoes National Park and take the night hike to where the lava flows into the ocean." He lowered his voice. "It is highly discouraged because it is so dangerous, but there's always a group of brave souls willing to take the chance with a local guide."

"The Park Service has rangers at the end of the road," Bob added, "but they won't stop you. Just be sure you wear sturdy shoes and bring a jacket, flashlight, and plenty of water."

"Did you take the hike also?" the other German woman, Margith, asked.

"Sure did," Bob answered, "but I couldn't get

Angie to go. Good thing too, 'cause it took four hours just to get to the lava flow. It was worth it, though." His eyes glittered. "Man, it was quite a sight."

Ingrid spoke up. "Lots of people hike it during the day, but it's much more dramatic to see the fiery flow in the dark."

"This all takes place at night and it's a four-hour hike?" Amalia asked in disbelief. "Then you had to hike back?"

Klaus answered her. "No, some choose to spend the night. It is quite something to sleep under the stars. Romantic, too." He kissed Ingrid. "We hiked back at five in the morning, before it got too hot."

Suddenly their tour guide clapped his hands to indicate it was time to pack up and head back down the mountain. Amalia rubbed her sore calves ruefully. She was not looking forward to the walk, but at least it was downhill. She smiled as Klaus helped her to her feet. She was so tired, she almost felt her progress over the last few months was all for naught. Still, the idea of the lava hike intrigued her, especially its forbidden aspect.

Chapter Four

Paige settled back in her airline seat for the thirty-minute flight to Kailua-Kona on the Big Island. Her few days checking out the university in Honolulu had been very productive. Besides the fact that anyone in their right mind would want to go there, the Ph.D. program was excellent. The dean had even indicated she stood a good chance of getting some type of scholarship. She'd been flattered to find out that he was even familiar with her thesis study.

She opened the map that the flight attendant had given her. He'd told her the drive to Volcanoes

National Park from where she was staying would take about two hours. She already had her reservations at the Volcano House Hotel, which overlooked Halema'uma'u Crater. She anticipated that her fellow travelers would be mostly straight families and honeymooners, as they were on this flight. And her gay guidebook listed only one bar on the whole island.

The plane took off, and it seemed she had just finished her complimentary macadamia nuts and guava juice when the announcement came to prepare for landing. Minutes later, they taxied down the runway of Keahole-Kona Airport and she exited from the plane by way of the stairs. The passengers all walked across the tarmac to the small open-air terminal, which seemed more like a train or bus station. There was a restaurant and bathrooms, a couple of gift shops, and several check-in counters. Their baggage arrived on one conveyor belt. As Paige waited for her suitcase, she checked out the other passengers. Like herself, they were all dressed in casual vacation clothes. Most of the men wore colorful Hawaiian shirts. They seemed to be mostly couples; she saw only three children. A few people appeared to be alone. Her gaze lingered briefly on one tall woman dressed in a traditional muumuu. She was much too skinny for Paige's taste, but strawberry-blonde hair framed a pretty face that showed her fatigue. When the woman pulled two big suitcases off the conveyor belt, Paige momentarily thought of offering her assistance, but then her own bag appeared. When she looked around, the woman had disappeared.

Paige crossed the street to the line of rental car counters. Several people were ahead of her, but she didn't have to wait long. Soon she was driving her rented four-wheel-drive Subaru away from the airport and onto Queen Kaahumanu Highway. She would be spending her first night in Captain Cook with a gay man named Mitch. He ran an informal B&B and came highly recommended by one of Rory's numerous friends. Mitch had told her he was less than an hour's drive from the airport.

Amalia didn't know how she lucked out, but no one was waiting in line when she got to the rental car counter. She'd opted for a mid-size sedan, and when she got in, it seemed much too luxurious. She and Kathy had both driven small foreign cars. The sedan handled well, though, and she felt more comfortable as she drove away from the airport. As she turned right off of the airport road and onto the main highway, she couldn't help but be surprised by the surrounding countryside. The tropical forest she expected was no-where to be seen. Instead, a barren vista stretched out all around her — a landscape of black lava with tall tufts of dried grass growing up through the cracks and boulders. Interestingly, the black rock was covered with graffiti created from what appeared to be pure white stones of different shapes and sizes. There were messages of greeting as well as farewell, love prose of all sorts, hearts with initials, and even images of people and animals. She marveled that they were left undisturbed, and she wondered where, amidst all this black lava, people found the white stones.

Just as she was beginning to wonder if she'd picked the wrong island, black lava gave way to lush vegetation, and then she was at the busy intersection of Queen Kaahumanu Highway and Palani Road in downtown Kailua-Kona. She turned left onto Palani and followed its winding trail up the steep hillside, feeling her ears pop at one point. She drove slowly to be sure not to miss her turnoff. The tree-lined driveway of the B&B was flanked by two stone posts connected with a white wooden gate now left open. She could see the white house through the trees. She drove around a small curve and parked the car. As she got out, her host came to greet her.

"*Aloha,*" he said, extending his hand and giving her a big grin, "I'm Scot. Welcome to Hale Kipa 'O Pele."

"Thank you," she replied and followed him to the house. A wooden lanai ran along its length. She could see herself spending many relaxing hours on the wicker couch and looking out over the lush landscape.

"We have a small orchard of mango trees," Scot said as he waved toward the trees. "The hot tub is right here. Please feel free to use it anytime." They stepped into the house and she followed him through the living room to a back bedroom. "This is the Ginger Room. I know you'll find it comfortable. If you give me your keys, I'll get your suitcases."

She plopped down on the bed and looked around with pleasure. She smiled to see the ever-present geckos on the walls. She'd had them in the motel on Oahu and had come to enjoy the clicking sounds they made. They helped keep the bugs at bay, she'd been told. A ceiling fan sent cooling air down on her.

Scot appeared with her suitcases. He left briefly and then returned with a plateful of sliced pineapple and a glass of freshly made iced tea complete with a sprig of mint. Amalia sipped the cold drink gratefully. "This is delicious," she said as she bit into a piece of juicy sweet fruit. The juice dribbled down her chin and she wiped it away with her hand. "A little messy." She laughed.

"I'll just set the plate down over here," Scot said as he put it on the dresser. "So, how did you hear about us?"

She smiled. "To tell the truth, I liked the picture of your place in the gay travel guide."

He smiled too. "That's always good to know. By the way, you'll be our only guest for a while."

"I think I'll like that better. I'm not really up for meeting lots of people right now."

If he was curious at her words, he didn't show it. "Got any plans for the afternoon?"

"I thought I'd unpack and then do a little window shopping."

"You'll want to take Palani Road and follow it down until it turns into Alii Drive. That's where all the little boutiques and such are located. It's right on Kailua Bay too. The sunset is extraordinary, and several restaurants have good views."

She felt a sharp twinge of sadness. Hawaii and its romantic sunsets were made for lovers, and she was here without hers. And it struck her suddenly that it was also Memorial Day. She felt the tears in her eyes and could only nod, hoping Scot would leave. He seemed to understand her need to be alone, for he smiled briefly and then left. She bit into another slice of pineapple, its tart sweetness more flavorful than any she'd tasted on the mainland. She couldn't help but think of Kathy, who'd resisted Amalia's attempts to feed her a more healthy diet. She'd been a steak-and-potatoes kind of gal, but Amalia thought even Kathy would enjoy this pineapple.

With a sigh, she turned to her suitcases. She unpacked quickly and decided to change from her muumuu into a new silk shorts set and go check out those restaurants that Scot had mentioned. At lunchtime, there would be no sunsets to remind her.

Paige couldn't believe that the two-lane highway she was on was the island's largest. After Kailua-Kona the traffic was practically nonexistent. Queen Kaahumanu Highway turned into Kuakini Highway, and Paige passed through several little towns, many of which didn't even have a traffic signal. The Pacific Ocean on her right appeared and reappeared, each time farther and farther away, as she traveled inland. The barren lava flows near the airport had given way to green rolling countryside. Having found the plane much too cold, she decided against using air conditioning. The tropical heat weighed on her like a blanket, but not unpleasantly so. And the earthy smells of dirt and vegetation mingled with the perfumed fragrance of flowers made an exotic combination for her to enjoy.

She arrived in the village of Captain Cook and followed the directions her host had given her. She smiled as she turned right at the Internet Café. So, even paradise wasn't immune to technological encroachment. She found Mitch's driveway. If she hadn't had the four-wheel drive, there was no way she could have made it down the almost vertical slope.

She parked next to a Jeep Cherokee and got out. Numerous pieces of snorkeling gear hung from the latticework walls of the garage. She grabbed her suitcase and climbed the stairs to the house.

Mitch greeted her at the door, reaching out to take her suitcase. He was tall and medium built, with reddish-blond hair and a mustache. Broad-shouldered, he wore a Hawaiian shirt and jeans. His laughing blue eyes and genuine smile made Paige feel right at home.

"Welcome to my home," he said. "You had no trouble finding it?"

"Your directions were perfect."

"Let me show you around." He led her into the house and then outside onto a balcony. She looked down and saw trees she'd never seen before. Mitch seemed to read her mind. "Those are mango trees," he said, pointing down the hill, "and those over there are coffee. I also have bananas growing somewhere."

"I've never tasted a mango."

"You're in for a treat then. I'll be sure to include it with your breakfast." He led her back inside. "Your room's this way. I don't put any restrictions on my guests, so please feel free to make yourself right at home."

"Are there any others staying?"

He put her suitcase next to the bed. "Oh no, I only have one at a time. I'm not your standard B and B." He winked. "That's why I'm so cheap."

Remembering that she hadn't seen any kind of shingle outside his house she said, "Yeah, my friend Rory said you just do this kind of on the side."

"A little extra cash here and there is good. I'm a Realtor in my day job."

"How'd you wind up here?"

"I just plain got tired of South Carolina. It was easy to transfer my Realtor license. Now, how about something to drink?"

Paige thought she had detected a slight accent. "Anything cold would be great."

"I'll be right back."

Deciding against unpacking, she followed him instead to the kitchen. The sound of the ice clinking in the glass and the carbonated hiss of a Pepsi made her realize just how thirsty she was. She hadn't stopped once on the way. She was also very hungry. "I passed a place on my way here — the Aloha Café. Is it any good?"

"It's terrific, if you like food on the healthy side. If you're looking for greasy burgers, it's not the place to go."

She leaned against the counter and took a big gulp of soda. "Sounds good to me. How far away from the volcano did you say you were?"

"It's about two to three hours' drive. Don't be fooled by the mileage signs. It might not be many miles away, but it's a slow trip. Route Eleven is no L.A. freeway. And you'll probably want to stop along the way. What kind of car did you rent?"

"A Subaru Outback."

He nodded appreciatively. "Then you might want to detour down South Point Road and visit Ka Lae, the southernmost point in the United States. You can't really get there with a regular car. And it's also where you'll find a green sand beach, if you're up for a six-mile hike."

"Green? I've heard of the black sand beaches, but not green."

"Yes, we have red too." He grabbed a jar full of differently colored layers of sand and handed it to her. "These colors come from the minerals collected by the lava as it moves toward the surface of the earth. When we have an eruption, the lava deposits those minerals and the sand is left with the resulting colors."

"That sounds really cool. I hope I have time to see it all."

"What's your schedule like?"

"My plan is to leave tomorrow for Volcanoes National Park. I've made reservations at the Volcano House Hotel. I've heard that I can take a hike out to where the lava still flows into the ocean."

"Yes. Can you believe Kilauea erupted in nineteen eighty-three and the lava is still flowing? The fire goddess Pele is a very busy lady." He motioned for her to follow him into the living room. "I don't know about this hiking business, though. It's extremely hazardous. People get lost or stranded out there all the time because they go without flashlights and don't understand the area."

"Well, I plan to go with an organized tour."

He laughed. "There's no such thing, honey. You'll need to find a local willing to take you, and there's a lot of preparation involved in making it safe."

She was disappointed. She thought it would as easy as signing up for a tour. "Well, is it hard to find someone?"

"I'll see what I can find out. You go ahead with your plans, and I'll contact you at the hotel. Just be careful and don't try anything on your own. Not that long ago, a couple of newlyweds fell into the ocean when a lava ridge collapsed, and they were never found."

Paige laughed nervously. "I get the point. I promise not to go alone."

"Good. Now, let me tell you about some of the things to do around here. You have to go to Pu'uhonua o Honaunau, the Place of Refuge. It's one of the most sacred of the ancient *heiau*, or temples. And of course, right here in Captain Cook we have the monument to Captain James Cook. He was killed in seventeen seventy-nine while trying to stop a fight between the Hawaiians and his men. We've also got several coffee plantations in the area."

She held up her hand in mock protest. "Wait! That's too much to absorb at once. Let me just do the volcano thing first, and then I'll see about the rest."

Mitch looked at his watch. "I've got some paperwork to catch up on, and then I'm free for the afternoon. How about I take you snorkeling after you get back from lunch?"

"It's a date."

After lunch at a Mexican restaurant, Amalia spent the entire afternoon exploring the shops and scenic spots along Alii Road, including the Mokuaikaua Church and the Hulihe'e Palace. She strolled down a path leading to Kailua Bay. The water looked enticing, and for a time she walked slowly along a small beach. She took off her sandals and sat on a large rock, letting the warm water lap gently against her feet. This was just the sort of vacation she and Kathy had dreamed about but could never afford. She felt the tears prickle her eyes again and wiped them away almost angrily. She cursed the drunk driver who had taken Kathy from her, and then felt ashamed to have such hostile feelings in this beautiful and peaceful place. It seemed to her suddenly that she could feel her aneurysm pulsing in her abdomen, a subtle reminder of her ordeal. She crossed her hands over her belly, took a few deep breaths, and felt calm once again.

The sun began to set, a huge orange ball of fire dipping slowly into the ocean. It took only minutes before it vanished into the horizon and darkness lay over her like a warm blanket. The raucous noise of birds settling into the tree behind her abruptly ceased with the disappearance of the sun. The sweet smell of plumeria drifted with the breeze, bringing a smile to her lips. Behind her, the street noises seemed muffled. The crunch of driftwood drew her attention as two lovers walked hand-in-hand along the sand. The woman laughed softly as the man pulled her into his arms for a deep kiss. Amalia couldn't help but watch them, but she didn't feel the twinge of envy she would have expected. Instead, she felt happy for them, and when they broke apart and came in her direction, she nodded and waved.

She slid off the rock, the warm sand clinging to her wet feet. She walked along the sidewalk back to her car, where she brushed the sand from her feet and put her sandals on. She stopped for carry-out Chinese and then drove back to the B&B. Scot's lover, Brent, was home.

"Hello, Brent," she said, holding out her hand. "I'm Amalia."

"*Aloha*," Brent replied. "How do you like Hawaii so far?" He motioned for her to sit down on the couch. "Would you like a TV tray?"

"I don't really want to eat dinner in your living room."

He waved a dismissive hand. "We do it all the time." He brought the tray over and opened it for her, then went to the kitchen for a napkin and a spoon. "So, what are your plans?"

"I've decided to go to the volcano park tomorrow. Scot was going to call and make reservations for me." She spooned rice and shrimp with lobster sauce onto her plate. "Would you like some? There's plenty."

"Thanks, but Scot and I have plans for dinner. Do you need a fork?" She held up her chopsticks and shook her head. "He left a message for you. You got the last room at the Volcano House Hotel. They must have had a cancellation."

"Great!" she replied. "Oh, in answer to your earlier question, I love Hawaii. Life seems to move much more slowly here. The frantic pace I'm used to is gone."

"I agree. Scot's originally from Oahu, but I moved here from Santa Fe and have never regretted it."

"Scot says you fly to Oahu every day?"

"Yes, I work for an accounting firm in Honolulu. Sometimes I work too late and have to stay overnight because the last flight out is at ten."

She laughed. "That half-hour commute you have by

plane is a lot shorter than mine was by car into D.C. Traffic jams, irate drivers. What a way to start the workday."

"What do you do?"

"I worked as a production assistant for a local television station before my accident. I haven't worked since." She took a bite of shrimp. "The insurance settlement was quite generous."

Just then, Scot came noisily into the house and practically dropped his grocery bags onto the breakfast bar that separated the kitchen from the living room. Brent joined him in the kitchen. "How did you like downtown Kailua?" Scot asked.

"Very nice. I was so happy to find a gallery featuring that photographer Kim Taylor Reece. I saw some of his photos at my motel on Oahu. His work is stunning."

"Yes, we've got his prints hanging around the house," Brent replied. "He really has captured the essence of the ancient hula."

The two men finished putting away the groceries. "We'll see you in the morning," Brent said as they headed out the door. "Feel free to use the house however you want. Maybe watch TV or try the hot tub."

"Thanks."

She finished her dinner and cleaned up. She didn't really feel like watching television, but perhaps a few minutes in the hot tub would relax her. She found a Loreena McKennitt CD among her hosts' collection and turned the volume on the player loud enough to hear outside. Since she was alone, she decided to be a little daring and got into the tub naked. The water seemed too hot at first, but she slowly lowered herself in, letting her body get used to the heat. She leaned back, feeling the water jet pulse against her lower spine. The warm, swirling bubbles caressed her skin. She closed her eyes and playfully let her legs float in front of her. Kathy's image hovered above her, but this time Amalia's eyes didn't well with tears.

Chapter Five

Paige woke early the next morning to the sound of rain. A tiny speckled gecko raced across the ceiling above her. She smiled at its antics. Mitch had told her his two cats killed most of the geckos unlucky enough to venture into the house. She was glad this one had escaped such a fate, at least for now. It was so tempting to just stay in bed, but she got up and took a quick shower. Her knapsack was already packed for a three-day, two-night stay at the national park.

Mitch was up and had coffee waiting. With the

first sip, she thought her taste buds had died and gone to heaven.

"This coffee is unbelievable. Is it the famous Kona coffee that I've heard so much about?"

He smiled. "Yes. I hope you like flavored coffees. The vanilla-macadamia nut is a favorite with my guests. I buy mine from the Ferrari Plantation. You can find Kona coffee everywhere on the island, but be careful when you buy it. If it says 'Kona blend,' you might be getting as little as ten percent pure Kona coffee."

"It has absolutely no aftertaste."

"That's because of our rich volcanic soil. If you leave a pot of Kona coffee on the burner all day, the last cup will taste as good as the first. No bitterness at all."

She finished her first mug of coffee and asked for another. Mitch brought over plates filled with muffins and fruit. "You said you'd never had mango so I sliced some up for you this morning."

She took a spear of the golden fruit. Both sweet and little tangy, it certainly beat the same old apples she ate back home. She selected a pineapple muffin from the plate.

"Those came from the Aloha Café," Mitch said as she took a bite. He pushed a piece of paper toward her. "Here's the name of the man to call about the lava hike. He's a local who comes highly recommended. My contacts tell me he will be going out tonight."

"Wow! That's fast work. You were going to call me at the hotel."

"It must be a sign that Pele is waiting for you. Honor her, and she will protect you."

She wiped the crumbs from her chin and swallowed the last of her coffee. "Thanks so much for everything," she said as she stood. "I've got your map too."

"One word of warning." Paige looked at Mitch, the seriousness of his tone setting off little alarm bells in her head. "Look at the volcanic rocks, but don't take any. That is considered to be very bad luck."

She smiled and nodded. She didn't really believe in all that bad luck nonsense, but she wasn't about to tell her host that. She resolved that if she did take any lava souvenirs, she certainly wouldn't tell him. Grabbing her knapsack, she headed to the car. The rain had stopped, and the sun shone through the breaking clouds. She drove with the windows open and decided the only stop she'd make along the way was to Ka Lae. The thought of green sand was just too much to resist.

Amalia couldn't believe it was raining when she woke up. The disappointment in her face must have been apparent when she went into the kitchen because Brent told her without being asked that it would stop by the time she finished breakfast. He'd made banana pancakes that morning and sliced up fresh papaya. The coffee was better than any she'd had before.

"Scot told me last night that you want to hike out to where the lava's flowing into the ocean. It's certainly exciting, but very dangerous." He gave her a slip of paper. "I checked with some friends of mine in Pahoa Village and they gave me the name of John Kamakau. It costs one hundred dollars cash, and you need to meet up with him at the bottom of Chain of Craters Road at about eight o'clock. If enough people show up, he'll take a group out. He does this all by word of mouth."

"Does he take people out every day?"

"No, but my friends are pretty certain he'll be there tonight. You can't really ask about it at the hotel. The National Park Service frowns on this sort of thing."

She finished up her pancakes before answering. "It's kind of thrilling, I think, to be doing something so dangerous and forbidden. It's almost too scary."

"It'll be a strenuous walk over rough terrain for several hours. You do have good hiking boots, don't you?"

"Oh, yes. Breakfast was delicious. *Mahalo.*" She pushed her empty plate away and stood up. "Guess I'd better get going. If I'm hiking tonight, I want to be sure I'm well rested. Thanks for all your help."

She grabbed her overnight bag and headed out to the car. She decided to stop in town and buy some food and water. Brent was right — it had stopped raining. A brilliant blue sky peeked through quickly disappearing white clouds. It was going to be a glorious day. Amalia felt happier than she had in a long while.

Amalia drove steadily along the winding road, passing through small towns and villages. She resisted the urge to stop and soon found herself entering Volcanoes National Park. She pulled to the side of the road and balanced her new camera precariously on the car's roof so she could take a picture of herself standing at the entrance sign made of big stones. She found herself laughing out loud as she raced over to the sign to get there before the camera shutter clicked. Well, if nothing else, she'd have an action shot of her backside.

She stopped at the Kilauea Visitor Center, which housed the small historical Jaggar Museum and showed films of recent volcanic eruptions. Before leaving, she learned that the park was not only America's oldest, but also encompassed two of the most active volcanoes in the world, Kilauea and Mauna Loa. Quickly tiring of the tourists, she gathered up some literature and drove the short distance to the hotel. After checking in, she ventured out behind the building. There, beyond the line of trees, lay a barren landscape leading to the dark outline of Halema'uma'u Crater from which came white puffs of smoke or steam. It looked like the impact point of a gigantic meteor.

She went back inside and decided to have lunch in the restaurant. She ordered the mahimahi special and settled back in her chair for a little people-watching. In the midst of all the honeymoon couples and tourist families with screaming children, she spotted a woman who immediately set off her gaydar. Tall, with dark blonde hair cut short, the woman followed the hostess to a table. Her stride was strong and confident. The waiter brought Amalia's lunch, but it sat untouched while she watched to see if someone joined the stranger. The woman suddenly looked up and caught Amalia staring. Quickly picking up her glass of iced tea, Amalia took a sip and then started on her lunch. She felt her cheeks grow warm with an embarrassed flush. God, it had been too long since she was with a woman. Kathy would have been the first to tell her to get out and find someone new. But it had been a long time since she'd felt attractive in any way, both because of her own physical problems and her grief. She gave a quick glance at the woman and was happy to see that she wasn't paying any attention. Perhaps she wasn't gay after all. Still, it was unusual to see a woman alone. Hell, what was she thinking? *She* was here alone, wasn't she?

She finished her lunch and made a quick exit. She wanted to visit Devastation Trail and then rest up in her hotel room later before heading down to the spot where Brent told her to meet this John Kamakau fellow. As she drove along Crater Rim Drive, she couldn't help but think of the lanky blonde with the tight ass and broad shoulders. In the deep recesses of her broken psyche, she felt the stirrings of a long-dormant desire.

Paige covertly watched as the woman who'd been eyeing her left the restaurant. She'd been startled when she'd looked up from her menu and caught her staring. The woman had been very careful not to look at Paige again. All through lunch, the feeling gnawed at her that the pretty face and strawberry-blonde hair were familiar. She was sure they'd met before, but where? It wasn't until the woman left the room that Paige remembered — she'd seen her yesterday at the airport in Kailua-Kona and had deemed her too skinny. She looked as tired today as she did then, and Paige wondered why she was here alone. A jilted bride perhaps? A harried mom escaping for a moment of peace while her family napped? A vacationing lesbian?

Now, *that* would be interesting. And what an odd coincidence that they were both staying at the hotel.

She finished lunch and decided to spend the hot part of the day writing postcards to send back home. She felt bad that she hadn't called Rory once in the six days she'd been in Hawaii. She also had to write her landlord and give the required month's notice. She figured by the time he got the letter, she'd owe another week's rent, so she enclosed a check. Rory would be happy for the extra time. She sent him a postcard of King Kamehameha and gave him the news. She also included Mitch's phone number. Her parents got a postcard of a lavender cattleya orchid. She debated whether to send one to Marianne. A photo of an erupting volcano seemed somehow appropriate, so she wrote a too-bad-you're-not-here type of message. If Marianne read between the lines, it was more like a you-fucked-up-bad missive. The way the whole affair had ended had only served to reinforce Paige's mistrust of women.

She went downstairs and tossed the postcards into the mail slot. For Marianne, it was the final farewell. Paige's last fleeting thought of Marianne's voluptuous body, dark unruly curls, and smoldering black eyes was replaced by a tall, thin strawberry-blonde with as-yet-unknown eyes. Somewhere in between rested two sisters with pale golden hair, long tanned legs, and eyes as blue as the Pacific Ocean. Paige sighed deeply. Five days without a woman seemed to her to be an awfully long time.

She went back to her room and changed into jeans, plain blue T-shirt, and her hiking boots. She grabbed a windbreaker and a flashlight and then headed for the car. It was time for a little exploring, and the steep drive down Chain of Craters Road seemed a good place to start. The map from the visitors' center told her there'd be interesting stops along the way. She bought water, chips, and cookies from the hotel gift shop. Sugar and salt — what a dinner combination, she thought as she threw the bag onto the seat of her Subaru.

Amalia woke with a start and then scrambled quickly out of bed when she saw the time. She'd napped a lot longer than she'd intended, but at least now she felt well-rested. The walk earlier along Devastation Trail was farther than she'd thought, but it had been fascinating. Created by a volcanic eruption in 1959, the burned and blackened countryside showed pockets of new life. Throughout the brown-black sand hills and valleys, wood charred pure white lay scattered like tossed bones. She'd heard creatures stirring in the sparse vegetation, but none showed themselves. The trail's path eventually led to a rain forest, but she'd cut short the hike to save her strength for the evening.

Now, she found herself driving away from the lush rain forests and down a steep and winding road that in several places gave her more than a twinge of fear as she observed the sheer drop-off.

The flashback came unexpectedly, brought on by the headlights of an approaching car that crossed the yellow line just a bit. As she instinctively swerved, the plunging drop evoked blurred images of terror and confusion. She could feel the sweat break out over her entire body as she suppressed a scream. Panic-stricken, she could swear she felt the icy water of the river engulf her. She stopped the car and leaned her forehead against the steering wheel, waiting for her breathing and heartbeat to return to normal.

It seemed an eternity, but in a few minutes she felt calm enough to continue her drive. She focused on the countryside of rippled, undulating lava flows gone black and hard with time. She stopped several times on the pretense of reading the informational signs that identified different eruption sites, but more to quiet her jangled nerves. The farther down she traveled, the more the wind seemed to pick up. She was glad she'd brought a jacket.

Amalia breathed a sigh of relief when she finally made it to the bottom of the road. Following others who had arrived earlier, she parallel parked the car on the shoulder and then walked to where the paved road ended abruptly, covered as it was by hardened lava stretching out as far as the eye could see. A prominent sign warned tourists about the dangers of attempting to walk out beyond what was considered safe. Besides the obvious ones, there was also the risk of exposure to poisonous gases.

A small wooden structure housed some informational literature and provided a meager shelter. It was already getting dark, but the shelter had no lights. Two park rangers were available to answer questions. They had set up a large telescope, and Amalia took a peek through its powerful lens. She couldn't help but gasp when she saw lava spurting fountainlike from what appeared to be a break in the mountain. Orange-gold in color, its dangerous beauty intensified as darkness descended.

"It must be amazing to see that up close," she commented to a female ranger who was eyeing her appreciatively. The attention made her feel good.

"Amazing yes, but also extremely hazardous. Only people who know what they're doing should try to approach, volcanologists and the like. The best way for tourists to see it really is to take one of the helicopter tours."

Amalia acknowledged the subtle warning with a nod. She returned the woman's gaze. The nametag on her crisp uniform read "Comstock." She toyed with the idea of forgetting the hike and asking Ranger Comstock to go out for a drink.

As if reading her thoughts, the woman said, "I only have to work about another hour. Perhaps I could show you the nightlife of Hilo later?"

Amalia felt her cheeks flush, a seemingly common occurrence lately. Grateful for the dusk, she replied, "Thanks, Ranger Comstock, but I already have plans for the evening. It's sweet of you to ask."

With obvious disappointment, Ranger Comstock smiled and said, "Perhaps another time. You're staying at the hotel, Miss . . . ?"

"My name's Amalia." She held out her hand. The ranger took it in a firm yet gentle grip. "Yes, I'm at the hotel, but only for two nights. I head back to Kailua-Kona on Thursday." She withdrew her hand and gestured toward the dark mountain. "That can't be where the lava hits the ocean?"

"Oh no. That's just a vent there. You can't see it from here." She pointed. "You have to head toward that billowing steam, but it's about four hours away on foot." She smiled. "I'm sure you won't be doing that."

"Thanks. I think I'll just walk out a teeny bit."

She turned and self-consciously defied the posted warning sign. She could see a few other people heading across the rock as well. Her instructions for meeting up with John Kamakau were to walk out about 500 yards and look for a Japanese lantern. She snapped on her flashlight and negotiated her way carefully across the creviced lava with its jagged chunks and sharp, stony boulders. She was glad she'd bought sturdy hiking boots. One twist of an ankle would end her adventure rather quickly.

By the time she saw the faint glow of the Japanese lantern, night had fallen completely. Overhead, the stars glittered whitely against a blue-black sky. A crescent moon shimmered pale yellow.

Up ahead, shadowy forms mingled, and she heard laughter and an occasional shriek. About ten people appeared to be gathered around the lantern. She looked at her watch in the glow of her flashlight. Eight o'clock on the nose. A tall, burly man drew their attention.

"*Aloha*, everyone," he said, his voice low but clear. "My name is John Kamakau, and I will be your guide tonight. I promise you a very exciting time, but I must warn you of a few things first." He handed out sheets of paper as he continued. "This is a very dangerous hike. We will be traveling across rough terrain in the dark. I have a powerful lantern, and I'm assuming you all have flashlights?" He waited while everyone gave murmured affirmations. "This paper I'm giving you is a waiver of responsibility. It just means that you or your families won't sue me if you are injured or killed. It states that you know the danger and have chosen to participate anyway." He paused for effect. "Also, we will probably walk for close to four hours to where the lava meets the sea. I will have friends with four-wheel drives waiting to bring us back. Now is the time to change your mind."

A high-pitched voice floated across the darkness. "Roger, maybe we should leave. We can just do the helicopter thing. Why do you have to be so close?"

The man's answering voice was harsh, impatient. "We've done everything you wanted on this vacation, Anne. Now it's my turn."

"Oh, like you don't get your way most of the time. You are so damned insensitive . . ."

Embarrassed, Amalia tuned out the quarreling couple and concentrated on filling out her waiver. When finished, she examined her fellow hikers. She counted three obvious couples, three men, and one other woman. When the woman gave her waiver to John, the lantern light revealed her to be the one she'd seen earlier that day during lunch.

Amalia couldn't help but smile again as she gazed over the woman's tight jeans and T-shirt, an unmistakably strong and muscular body. She'd tied a white windbreaker casually around her narrow waist and slim hips. The wind ruffled her short hair into cute little tufts that Amalia would bet the woman would hate if she knew about. As Amalia approached John and turned in her waiver, she felt the woman watching her.

Chapter Six

Sensing someone's gaze, Paige looked up and
spotted the woman from the hotel. This was the
second time she'd been under her scrutiny and the
third time she'd noticed her. Well, she wasn't about to
let an opportunity slide by again. She strode
purposefully toward her.

"Hi there. My name's Paige Parker. You here
alone?"

The woman tilted her head slightly. In the faint
glow of the lantern light, her blonde hair gleamed
with a reddish tint. She offered her hand, which Paige

took. The skin was baby soft, making her want to kiss it. On impulse, she did just that.

"Amalia Grant, and yes, I'm here alone."

"Boyfriend troubles?"

Amalia laughed. "Why no, Miss Parker, I'm sure you know that's not the reason."

"What's this Miss Parker stuff?"

"Okay then, Paige."

"Since you're here alone, how'd you like a hiking companion?" She didn't add that Amalia looked like she needed one. Really, the woman was entirely too thin. Remembering how tired she'd looked, Paige wondered if she'd been ill.

"That would be nice." Amalia smiled a bit ruefully. "To tell you the truth, I'm not sure I'm up to this hike. It depends on how fast John expects us to go."

Paige felt a twinge of irritation. Was this woman going to hold them up, or worse, force them to cut the hike short? "Then maybe you shouldn't go."

She winced when she saw the expression on Amalia's face. Her tone must have been harsher than she intended. Then Amalia's mouth tightened with determination.

"I'll be just fine."

"Look, I didn't mean to imply anything, but you don't exactly look like the athletic type." Right after she said it, she wished she hadn't. Sometimes she had no tact. It was a flaw that came to haunt her again and again. She found herself apologizing.

"I'm not offended," Amalia said, "but I am a lot stronger than I look. As a matter of fact, I hiked to the summit of Diamond Head just this past weekend."

Just then, John clapped his hands. "I think we're ready to start now. One more reminder, your cost for this little excursion is one hundred dollars per person. You should have been informed of that by whomever gave you my name, but sometimes these little details slip." He looked around the group. "Everyone okay with that?"

Nine heads all nodded in unison. Roger and Anne, the quarrelers, had chosen to leave and were already out of sight. John came around and collected the money, and then they started the trek.

They picked their way over the hardened lava. John's little group was not the only one out that night. In the distance, other dark forms moved slowly across the devastated countryside, all in search of the adrenaline rush that would come from standing so close to death. Paige had no idea what to expect when they got to the lava flow. The films at the park's visitor center showed a fiery river of molten gold that bubbled and pulsed down its path to the ocean, where it would meet the cold water with a loud hiss of smoke and steam spiraling into the sky.

John's voice floated over the air to them. "In January of nineteen eighty-three, Kilauea, the earth's most active volcano, erupted. What we are going to see tonight is a lava flow that spews from a satellite cone called the Pu'u O'o vent. Each year, lava adds hundreds of acres to Hawaii's land mass, but it will take thousands of years before you see this land covered with rain forest. Scientists estimate that the newest Hawaiian island, Loihi, won't emerge from the sea for another twenty thousand years."

"Someone told me there are two kinds of lava," one of the hikers said.

"They're right." John pointed his flashlight to the ground. "*Pahoe-hoe* is this smooth, ropey-looking lava.

67

It is hotter and contains more gases than the jagged and clinkery `a`a, which you will also find here. And speaking of lava, one of the more interesting sights to see at the park is the four-hundred-and-fifty-foot Thurston lava tube. These tubes are formed when . . ."

Paige tuned out his voice and concentrated on the woman beside her. Amalia walked briskly, almost too fast. It was as if she was trying to prove something. Paige touched her lightly on the arm. "This isn't a race, you know."

Amalia slowed. She kept her eyes down, presumably to follow the path of her flashlight. A good idea, Paige thought when she herself tripped. It would be hard to hold a conversation with one's head bent, but it was necessary. No wonder this hike lasted four hours.

"I guess I'm just trying to prove something to myself," Amalia said so quietly that Paige had to move closer to hear. Their arms brushed. Paige, still jacketless, felt a shiver run up her body. "I've been working real hard to get back into shape," Amalia continued. "You see, I was in a bad car accident, and I've spent nearly two years in physical therapy."

"Do you want to talk about it?"

Amalia laughed without humor. "That's part of my therapy too. I'm actually doing quite well now. I just have periods of extreme tiredness." She glanced at Paige. "Do you really want to hear this?" Paige nodded. "Kathy and I were coming home from visiting her sister in the hospital. Claire had just given birth to a baby girl. Kathy was ecstatic to be an aunt."

As Amalia fell silent, Paige took her hand and gave it a reassuring squeeze. As she tried to then take her hand away, Amalia grabbed it and held on. They continued their careful steps across the hardened lava, which reminded Paige of photos of the lunar landscape. She looked ahead. John and the others weren't too far away.

As if he'd sensed her concern, his voice rang out. "Everyone okay back there?"

There was a chorus of yeses and then only the sound of boots crunching against rock. Someone asked a question, and John's voice droned on. When Amalia started talking again, she sounded almost dreamlike.

"We were driving home along a quiet stretch of road. We'd bought an old farmhouse in the country outside Frederick, Maryland. It was late. Suddenly, there were headlights coming right at us. Kathy had nowhere to go. The car hit us head-on, and we plunged off the road down an embankment and into the river. I don't really remember the details. Just the lights and the pain. When I woke up, I was in a hospital and Kathy was dead."

Paige felt a shiver again, but this time it was from horror. She didn't know what to say, but she wanted to pull Amalia into her arms and soothe away the hurt. The silence stretched out.

"What happened to the other driver?" she finally asked softly.

"Oh, he lived. Young guy who'd had too much to drink. He was very arrogant at the trial. No remorse. He got two years for vehicular manslaughter and was out after six months."

"That's awful!" Paige said in outrage.

Amalia smiled bitterly. "His insurance company paid well, though."

"I take it you were badly hurt?"

Amalia nodded and spoke like she was reciting a

shopping list. "Broken legs and pelvis. Ruptured spleen and lacerated liver. A cracked vertebrae that caused bleeding in my spinal cord." She continued sarcastically, "I'm sure I was a good study for some medical student."

"You still have pain now?" Paige couldn't even begin to imagine what Amalia had gone through. She'd broken an ankle one time while rollerblading and thought that was bad enough.

"Some. I wasn't conscious for the most excruciating part of it all. Bleeding in my head caused seizures, so they put me into a phenobarbital coma to stop them. Guess that lasted two to three weeks."

"Seizures?" Paige croaked. This was sounding more and more like something out of a Robin Cook novel.

Amalia looked at her and gave her hand a reassuring squeeze this time. She laughed. "Don't worry, I'm not going to have one now. I do have an abdominal aortic aneurysm, though." Paige felt the blood drain from her face. "Don't look so alarmed, Paige. It's nothing to be concerned about. Let's talk about something else. What do you do?"

She took a couple of deep breaths. Yeah, right. Change the subject just like that. Still, she decided to honor Amalia's request even though she was dying from curiosity. She wondered if she'd ever hear the whole story. And she wanted to know more about Kathy. Was she Amalia's lover?

"I just got my master's in marine biology. I'm here because the University of Hawaii invited me to check out their Ph.D. program. I think I'll be staying."

"That's wonderful. Do you have a specialty? You know, like saving sea turtles or studying coral reefs?"

"I'm partial to whales. It's too late to see them now, but humpbacks come to Hawaii in late December until about April. I'd like to study them, I think."

"Oh, darn! I wanted to go on a whale-watch cruise. I read about some guy in Kailua-Kona who's got quite a reputation."

"You must be talking about Captain Dan McSweeney. Well, you can still take the cruise. There are plenty of other types to see now — pilot, sperm, and false killer whales. And you're sure to always see dolphins."

Amalia stopped abruptly, her breathing ragged. "I'm sorry. I've got to sit down for a minute. How long have we been walking?"

Paige looked at her watch. "A little over an hour."

Amalia rubbed her eyes. "I think I'm getting a headache from concentrating so much on the ground. And I suddenly feel very tired. I don't know if I can go on."

"Here, you rest for a minute." She put her jacket on a semiflat boulder and helped Amalia sit down. She then raced to catch up with the rest of the group. No one else seemed inclined to stop.

"John," she called out. He halted and turned. "One of your hikers is unable to continue."

The others in the group let out a collective groan. Brushing aside her own disappointment, Paige volunteered to return to the starting point with Amalia.

"You don't mind going back alone?" he asked.

"No sense in ruining it for everyone else." She looked over at Amalia's forlorn figure. "She's been ill. I guess she wasn't as recovered as she thought."

"Well, let me refund your money."

"Don't worry about mine. Keep it for your trouble. I'll just take Amalia's to her."

"If you're sure . . ." She nodded and he counted out the money. "Sorry you have to miss it. I'll be going out again on Saturday."

"Thanks. I'll probably just hire a helicopter."

Reluctantly, she watched as the rest of group continued on, the beams of their flashlights bobbing along the dark rock like corks in water. With a sigh, she turned back to Amalia. It was going to be a long trip back.

Amalia felt terribly guilty. She should have realized the hike would be too much for her. What could she have been thinking? Her trip to Diamond Head had worn her out, and that was a three-hour trek in the daylight. Plus, she'd only let three days pass between hikes.

She watched as Paige spoke with John. In the light of his powerful lantern, she saw what appeared to be an exchange of money. She should have told her not to get a refund. The others headed out while Paige stood silhouetted against the dark sky. She had a wonderful body — strong and tall. Her broad shoulders were straight, her bearing almost military. She reminded Amalia just a bit of Kathy, but she decided it was their similar hair colors. Paige was boyish, where Kathy had been shorter, fuller, and well-endowed.

She shook her head. She shouldn't be comparing women to Kathy. They hadn't spoken of it, but she was sure Paige was a lesbian. If she truly would be attending school here, it seemed possible that they could become friends. The idea made her think about the ones she had left behind in Maryland. She really missed Alexander. He could always make her laugh, even when she felt like dying.

Paige reached her, sat down, and clicked off her flashlight. She tried to hand over the refund money, but Amalia shook her head. "No, you keep it. It's the least I can do."

They sat companionably in the darkness. The wind off the invisible ocean felt cool and refreshing. If she strained, she thought she could hear the waves. It seemed as if she and Paige were the only people on earth.

Finally, she leaned over and whispered in Paige's ear. "I'm so very sorry to ruin your evening. It's awfully nice of you to help out a stranger."

She caught a faint whiff of Paige's cologne. Odd that she hadn't noticed it before. She reached up and stroked Paige's cheek. Propelled by some unknown force, she edged closer as Paige turned to look at her. Their eyes met and locked. She felt a tremor in her body, an almost physical pain of longing.

As if sensing her need, Paige leaned forward and gently kissed her. Amalia took her head in her hands and held her for a longer kiss. Their tongues met. The sensation almost made Amalia cry out. When Paige grabbed her arms and held her tightly, she welcomed the pain. It meant she was coming alive again. She could feel need and want and desire. And right now she desired this woman like no other.

Paige pushed her down against the hard rock. It bit into her back, but she didn't care. Paige's mouth was firm and insistent. Her tongue thrust deeply, eliciting a moan from Amalia. Her touch burned a path along Amalia's arms and breasts and thighs. She silently cursed the jeans she wore, wanting to feel Paige's fingers against her bare flesh. Almost frantically, she ran her hands along Paige's muscular arms, firm chest, and taut stomach. Her skin felt on fire. She pulled her own T-shirt off, urging Paige's mouth to her breasts. Paige suckled her nipples through the bra and then pulled it aside to take them one by one into her mouth.

"Oh God, Paige! I want you to make love to me." The plea came unbidden to her lips.

When Paige kissed her sensitive neck, Amalia thought she would pass out. Paige's hands crept down to the buttons of Amalia's jeans. Suddenly, through the red-hot haze of her passion, Amalia heard voices. She opened her eyes briefly and saw pinpricks of light bouncing toward them. She pushed Paige away.

"What the hell —"

"I'm sorry. I'm sorry, but people are coming." She pointed.

Paige followed the line of her finger. "Damn!"

With shaking fingers, Amalia fixed her bra and pulled her T-shirt back on. In the sobriety of the moment, she wondered how she could ever have let this happen. She was acting like some sex-crazed high school kid. She took a couple of deep breaths and smoothed down her hair before scrambling to her feet, standing on trembling legs. She switched on her flashlight just as four people came over a mound and bore down on them.

"Hey there!" a man's voice called out cheerfully. "Been to the lava yet?"

Beside her, Paige stood up too. "No, we couldn't go all the way," Amalia answered, thinking all the while that the words she'd spoken took on a double meaning.

"I told you it was too long a hike," a woman's strong Midwestern accent scolded as the four of them approached the two women. "And those park rangers said it was illegal."

"Oh hush, Charlotte," answered a man with an equally strong Midwestern accent. "I knew we should have taken the truck."

"You probably would have gotten stuck," Paige volunteered.

"Should we go back?" the cheerful man asked.

Amalia tensed, dreading the answer. What if they wanted to walk back with them?

Midwestern accent this time. "I want to go a little farther."

"Good luck," Amalia said hurriedly and grabbed Paige's hand. "C'mon, let's go." Heedless of loose rocks, she led them quickly over the lava before the four hikers could change their minds. She didn't slow down until the group was completely out of sight.

"That was a close call," she said a little breathlessly.

She could hear the laughter in Paige's voice when she answered. "It certainly would have given them something to write home about. Talk about your volcanic eruptions..."

Amalia giggled and then became self-conscious. "I don't normally do that sort of thing. Actually, I've never done it. I don't know what you must think of me."

"I think you're a passionate woman who's been

without a lover's touch for too long." She leaned over and kissed Amalia's cheek. "And I'd like to continue what we started when we get back to the hotel."

Amalia shook her head. "I don't think so. Not tonight. Please understand."

If Paige was disappointed, she didn't show it. "Can we at least get together for breakfast tomorrow?"

"I'd like that. In fact, if you don't have any real plans for tomorrow, maybe we could do some exploring together? I'd like to walk across the crater."

Paige laughed. "Oh no, no more strenuous walking for you. I'm making it my official duty to see to it that you don't overdo it again."

The idea of Paige acting as her guardian angel gave her a warm tingle. They held hands the rest of the way back, with Paige using her more powerful flashlight to light the way. Few cars remained parked on the road. The little shelter was closed up tight, and Ranger Comstock and her telescope were long gone. Amalia squinted into the darkness, looking in the direction of the lava spurt she'd seen earlier. She thought she glimpsed a faint glowing dot, but she knew it was impossible to see with the naked eye. They walked to Amalia's sedan.

With an exhausted sigh, she turned once more to Paige. "I want to say again how sorry I am that I cut short your hike. I'm just glad you were willing to come back with me so I didn't ruin it for everyone else too."

"Well, I couldn't have you walking back alone." She squeezed Amalia's hand. "I'm sure you'll find some way to reward me."

"Thanks again. I'll see you at breakfast."

Chapter Seven

The next morning they had breakfast together and then decided to explore the area some more. It had rained during the night, and the air was humid and heavy, a precursor to another hot day. The rain forest enclosed them in a luxuriant green cocoon of cool, earthy dampness with exotic smells and sounds. Dainty orchids of lavender and white provided delicate color in the verdant forest of majestic tree ferns, soft mosses, trailing vines, tall grasses, and other trees that Amalia couldn't even begin to name.

They wandered slowly through the forest on

narrow, winding dirt paths worn down by the trampling of thousands of feet. Amazingly, they didn't meet any other hikers. At several points along the trails, they found themselves overlooking sweeping vistas of desolation or deep volcanic craters still showing puffs of steam coming from fissures in their surfaces. Occasionally they would see tiny moving dots that turned out to be people crossing a crater. Paige knew Amalia really wanted to be down there with them, but they had agreed it would be too much for her. They were relatively cool and comfortable in the wet shelter of the rain forest, but the crater afforded no such refuge from the relentless sun.

"Oh, look," Amalia said, pointing to a moss-covered rock that jutted about eight inches high through matted leaves on the dirt path. "It has a little face, just like those totems they show in the brochures."

Paige didn't know what totems she was talking about, but she looked at the rock. A face did seem to peer at them through the mossy covering. It was actually kind of interesting. "You want me to take a picture?" she asked as she readied her camera.

"Yes, please."

Paige knelt down on one knee and focused her camera. She pressed the button, but nothing happened. Frowning, she checked to be sure the camera was turned on and the film had advanced. Yes to both. She pressed the button again. Nothing.

"I don't know what's wrong with this," she complained. "I took a photo not fifteen minutes ago when we saw that red bird." She shook the offending device.

"Maybe it's an omen. We're not meant to take its picture. Some things are sacred, you know."

Paige rolled her eyes and stood up. "Yeah, whatever."

"Are you a spiritual person?"

Paige continued on the path ahead. "I was raised Presbyterian, but I don't really understand the concept of God. I do know I don't believe in hokey superstitions."

"What's hokey to you may be serious to others. You should be careful what you say."

"I'm sorry if I've offended you."

"No, but I do respect the beliefs of others. The Hawaiians are a very spiritual people, and I won't take a chance in offending their gods, either the ancient ones or the Christian one."

Paige felt sufficiently chastised. She certainly hadn't expected a lecture this morning. She looked at her watch. Morning? Hell, it was already early afternoon. They'd been walking almost three hours. She took a deep drink of her bottled water, then paused on the path a moment. She pointed to the discreet wooden sign that directed them back to the hotel.

"It's past lunchtime. What say we head back to eat and then maybe go into Hilo this afternoon?"

"Lunch sounds good, but I don't think I'm interested in going to Hilo during the day. I'd like to visit Akaka Falls, which is north of the city."

"That sounds good to me," Paige said, wondering when *her* vacation had turned into *their* vacation, but not really minding. After all, it wasn't as if Amalia had forced her to spend time with her. And after last night, the cute blonde had certainly spiked her interest.

They'd also discovered over breakfast that they

were staying in B&Bs thirty minutes apart. She told Amalia about snorkeling with Mitch and invited her to come along the next time. Amalia in turn told her about a nighttime snorkeling or scuba dive where they could swim with manta rays. For someone who'd suffered the way she had, Amalia sure seemed anxious to do a lot of strenuous physical activity. Paige grinned. She hoped Amalia would be interested in the kind of physical activity they'd started last night.

As they approached the hotel, Amalia spoke. "Maybe you're right. I think Hilo might be a good idea for this afternoon. If we go to the falls, we'd just be backtracking to return to the hotel. We can visit them on our way home."

Paige nodded, thinking all the time that Rory would surely have a good laugh over this whole situation. Her time in Hawaii had turned out to be a lot more interesting than she'd expected. First the twins on Oahu and now this intriguing woman with the tragic past. Paige figured if anyone could help Amalia forget Kathy, she certainly could. In fact, she would bet on it. And she had the whole summer to do it.

The afternoon in Hilo had been pleasant. Amalia had enjoyed playing tourist, and Paige had seemed to like it too. They'd visited the stunning Rainbow Falls, as well as the historic downtown area. Paige had even tried her luck moving the Naha Stone, which legend held that Kamehameha the Great had moved as a teen, thus prophesying his rule of the islands. The story reminded Amalia of the legend of King Arthur who, as a child, removed the famed Excaliber from its granite sheath.

As evening shadows draped across the room, Amalia dressed for dinner in a rose and white silk sarong she'd bought that afternoon. She brushed her hair until it shone, and applied minimal makeup. She examined herself critically in the mirror. She was definitely putting on weight, and her legs were quite shapely from all the walking she'd been doing. The sarong accentuated her narrow waist and the curve of her hips. She brushed a touch more slate-blue shadow across her eyelids to give them a smokey effect and added mascara. For the first time in years she actually felt attractive. It was kind of exciting to be going on a real date.

She and Kathy had dated, but that would be nearly eight years ago. She had been all of nineteen, but Kathy was her fourth lover. The longest of the other three had only lasted one year, and a turbulent one at that.

She'd been lucky, too, that her parents were so understanding when she'd come out to them. She'd attributed it to the fact that both were heavily involved in amateur theater. Consequently, there'd always seemed to be lots of gay people at the house. Their full support had helped her through the trauma of Kathy's death.

She took a deep breath to ease her nervousness and turned from the mirror to leave her room. She was meeting Paige in the front lobby. Paige had refused to tell her where they were going, only that she should dress up. When she glimpsed Paige waiting, the sight made her stop in her tracks. Despite the warm weather, Paige wore tight black leather pants and a black button-down shirt, both of which suggested every curve, muscular or otherwise. Her dark blonde hair was feathered back from her face in a style reminiscent of the disco age. Small gold hoops in her ears caught the light. With her black leather jacket dangling nonchalantly over one shoulder and one black-booted foot resting against the railing in front of the reception counter, Paige flirted shamelessly with the Hawaiian clerk. Amalia felt a pang of jealousy and a flash of insecurity.

Just as Amalia was debating whether or not to return to her room, Paige turned around and smiled at her. Amalia felt mesmerized by those deep brown eyes as Paige came toward her, still grinning.

"You look positively stunning," Paige said as she kissed Amalia lightly on the cheek and draped an orchid lei around her neck.

Amalia breathed in the perfume of the lovely lavender blooms. "Thank you. You look great too, but aren't you hot?"

Paige's grin got wider. "Why yes, as a matter of fact, I am. But not because of the weather or my clothes." She winked.

Amalia felt her cheeks flush. The light scent of Paige's cologne swirled around her, making her almost dizzy. Or was it just the close proximity of their bodies? "Let's get going," she said.

"I've picked out a special place not too far from here. I wish we would be overlooking the ocean, but we'll save that for another time."

It gave Amalia a good feeling to think there would be another time. Paige held her hand to help her into the car, her touch electric. Unexpectedly, as Paige leaned across to lock the seat belt for her, Amalia was consumed with a rush of desire so intense it was almost painful. She took a deep breath, remembering that her attraction for Kathy had been as instantaneous.

Despite her inner turmoil, Amalia had a wonderful time at dinner. The restaurant was elegant but not stuffy. She ordered sea scallops of a size she'd never seen before. Lightly sautéed in a macadamia butter sauce, they practically melted in her mouth. The broccoli side dish, fresh and steamed to perfection, was sprinkled with slivered almonds. Paige ordered fish baked in coconut milk, along with Hawaiian sweet potatoes and cucumber Namasu.

She found herself laughing at Paige's stories of her Aunt Maggie and growing up gay in Iowa. She could easily visualize a young Paige in her cowboy outfit with the "real" cowboy boots.

"Are you still in touch with your aunt?" she asked.

Paige shook her head. "I called Ma before I came here to ask if she knew where Aunt Maggie was. No one seems to know, but I suspect she's happy."

"With the truck driver?"

Paige laughed heartily. "Her, or someone else, I'm sure."

Amalia bit into another succulent scallop. "So, she helped you come out?"

"I wish." Paige frowned. "Actually, the woman who brought me out was seventeen years older than me. She was my best friend's mother."

"Ouch." She was tempted to take her hand, but the look in Paige's eyes had shut her out.

"Let's just say she used me for her own purposes and didn't look back." She smiled again. "But what about you? Tell me about Amalia. I'd like to hear more about the accident and Kathy, if it's not too painful to talk about."

Amalia leaned back in her chair and took a sip of her rosé. She could tell the subject of the older woman was a painful one and decided to honor Paige's unspoken wish. "Well, I told you most of it last night. My injuries were pretty severe, but two years of physical therapy have worked wonders. I was a pretty good athlete before the accident, and I'm working my way back up."

"How long had you and Kathy been together?"

"Six years. We met our junior year in college and dated for a while at first. She was my fourth real girl-friend." She took another sip of wine. "We had such hopes and dreams. We bought this old farmhouse together that was in horrible shape. It took every penny we had. No more dinners out; we waited for movies to come out on video. We'd only been living there about eight months . . ."

"Did you stay in the house after Kathy died?"

"When I was strong enough to live on my own, yes. I've spent the last few months doing the reno-vations with the help of some friends. The house turned out quite lovely." She felt the momentary prick of tears and blinked them away. "I sold it the day I left for Hawaii."

"Sold it? But why?"

"I fulfilled Kathy's and my wish, but I didn't want to live there without her. Besides, it was time for a new life. I felt smothered by well-meaning friends and family. I had to prove to them and myself that I could make it on my own — that I was finally okay." She laughed without humor. "I don't mean on my own financially. That's something I don't have to worry about anymore. The accident settlements were generous."

"So, you left no one behind?"

Amalia smiled. "Not romantically, but lots of good friends." She lightly touched Paige's hand. "I expected Hawaii to bring me new happiness."

Paige took her hand. "I'd certainly like to try and help that along."

"I was hoping you'd say that."

Paige motioned for the waiter. "Ready to go back to the hotel?"

After paying, they left the restaurant. It was still very warm outside. Paige put her leather jacket in the back seat. Amalia had to admit that Paige made an awfully handsome butch in black. She exuded confidence and a little bit of arrogance as well, but it suited her. Amalia knew that Paige was a take-charge sort of gal, and the idea of it made her flush with anticipation. That she felt so strongly for someone she'd just met only made it more exciting. She smiled as she thought about what Alexander would say. He'd always told her that she was too conservative, that as much as he loved Kathy, he wished Amalia had played around more in the "bloom" of her youth.

Back at the hotel, Amalia suddenly felt nervous. "Can we go for a walk?" she asked as Paige helped her out of the car.

"Sure."

It was a lovely night. The sky was clear, the stars twinkling brightly against its deep black velvet. All around them, the air smelled earthy and rain forest damp. The creatures of the night serenaded them with a cheerful symphony of chirps, clicks, and buzzes. Paige took Amalia's hand in her own as they wandered in silence along a dimly lit path.

"I'd like to get to know you better," Paige finally said, her tone of voice making no mistake about just what she meant.

Amalia felt a little thrill, as well as a hint of anxiety. It had been two years since a woman had touched her. What would Paige think when she saw the scars? Would she think her too thin? She had to level with herself, though. She really wanted this woman, wanted to feel desired again, even if only for a moment. Who knew what the future would bring? Right now she knew only that she would give Paige what she wanted.

She reached up and pulled Paige to her. Their lips met, the kiss gentle at first, then more urgent. Paige's hands felt hot against Amalia's bare shoulders as she pressed Amalia tightly to her, crushing her lei. Their breathing quickened. Amalia slid her hands down to Paige's leather-clad ass. The leather felt smooth and surprisingly cool.

Paige kissed her neck and whispered in her ear, "Let's go to my room."

Amalia nodded and quickly found herself in Paige's room, which was identical to hers. In the darkness, Paige made short work of Amalia's sarong. It came off in one fluid movement, leaving her clad only in white satin bikini underwear. The strapless sarong had made wearing a bra unnecessary. She, in turn, stripped off Paige's leather pants, revealing long, muscled legs. Paige went to turn on the light, but Amalia stopped her.

"But I want to see you," Paige countered.

"I'm afraid," Amalia whispered, her confidence fleeing like leaves on the wind.

"I won't hurt you. I know it's been a while . . ."

Amalia silenced her with a kiss. "I'm afraid you won't like my body. That you'll think I'm ugly."

"I don't think that at all," Paige protested.

Paige stroked her arm, running her fingers along Amalia's sensitive shoulders and down over her breasts. Her nipples hardened, whether from a chill or Paige's touch, she couldn't be certain. Paige kissed her neck, and then took a nipple into her mouth. The feeling just about made Amalia pass out. A moan came from somewhere deep inside her.

She felt Paige stiffen when her hand slid over Amalia's stomach. With a sigh, she reached over and turned on the light. She may as well let Paige see everything. Paige gasped in the revealing light.

"It's the aortic aneurysm I told you about. It sometimes pulses like this, but it's nothing to worry about." She took Paige's hand and led it down the long scar that bisected her body. "This came from my surgeries."

"I . . . I'm so sorry. I can't believe I acted so stupid." Her face was red with embarrassment.

"It's all right. Do you want me to leave?"

Paige stared hard into her eyes. "Hell no! I'm not that shallow."

Amalia smiled and reached up to pull her down for another kiss. "I'm so glad," she murmured, running her hands through Paige's thick hair. She turned her head so Paige would kiss her neck. The touch of her hands made goose bumps rise on Amalia's arms and her scalp tingle.

It had been so long since she'd been touched, she

almost wanted to cry from the sheer pleasure of it. Paige's skin felt smooth and warm; her body was firm. They caressed each other and kissed for what seemed like hours before Paige finally lowered herself between Amalia's easily spread legs. Her fingers dipped deep, making Amalia gasp. Her tongue brought ripples of ecstasy coursing through Amalia's body. Though they were far from the ocean, she felt as if she drifted on waves, first lapping gently against the sand and then gathering speed and height as they crashed in a storming crescendo onto the shore. Her legs tensed and she drew her knees up, then pressed Paige's mouth into her, feeling her tongue move faster and her fingers go ever deeper. She grabbed Paige's hair.

"Oh, Paige," she whispered raggedly.

Paige licked her lightly and then came up to rest beside her. Amalia felt safe in her arms, keeping still while she caught her breath. Neither one spoke. With a sudden surge of energy, Amalia sat up and leaned over Paige's body, letting her fingers slide over Paige's breasts and smooth taut belly, between her muscular legs. Paige closed her eyes and moaned softly, thrusting her hips slightly forward. With a smile, Amalia let her mouth follow the path of her fingers.

Light would be peeking through the gaps in the drapes before the two would finally fall asleep.

Chapter Eight

Paige stretched and reached out for the woman sleeping beside her. Amalia had been a very responsive lover. As she pulled the naked woman close, she couldn't help but feel protective. She winced, thinking of the angry scar that marred Amalia's chest and belly. She couldn't even begin to imagine the pain she must have endured. She traced her fingers lightly across the other, more faded scars. Amalia stirred but did not wake. Paige continued caressing her gently and then took a lock of silken hair in her hand. Bone straight and soft as satin, it was a shade of pale blonde with just a hint of red. Paige smiled. She always did have a thing for blue-eyed blondes. The raven-haired Marianne had been a departure from her usual type. Come to think of it, she had been a departure in a lot more ways than hair color. She'd been sexually conservative, or so she'd led Paige to believe. Paige grimaced, remembering the scene with Richard and the dildo on the bed.

"What's wrong?"

Paige shook the memories from her mind and smiled at the woman who looked up at her with a worried frown. "Oh, nothing. Just thinking of something back home."

"Something or someone?"

Paige kissed the tip of her nose. "Okay, Miss Curious, it was someone, but no one you need to concern yourself with. She was inconsequential."

Amalia stiffened. "Is that how you'll describe me?"

"Of course not. Why would you think that?"

"I don't even know if I'll see you after today. Maybe I'm just a one-night stand."

Paige squirmed uncomfortably. Amalia read her a lot more accurately than she'd like. "Well, I won't deny that I've had one or two, but I promise you're not going to be one of them."

"Should I be worried?"

"Worried?"

Amalia sat up and looked at her seriously. "About HIV."

Paige flushed guiltily, thinking of the twins in Honolulu. Rory had taught her to know better. She'd been tested in the early days of her relationship with Marianne, and given what she'd learned about Marianne's relationship with Richard, it would probably be a good idea to get to a clinic as soon as possible.

"I'm sorry, Amalia. I honestly don't think you have anything to worry about, but I should have been more responsible."

"Well, it was my responsibility too. I guess I've just never had to think about it. I mean, I was monogamous with Kathy those six years and then celibate these last two." She smiled, but Paige could tell she was concerned.

"I'll get tested as soon as we get back. I'm sure Mitch will know where I can go."

Amalia looked at the clock and leaped naked out of bed. "Well, we'd better get dressed. We only have an hour until checkout. I'll meet you in the lobby."

Paige leaned back against the pillows and admired Amalia's sleek body before it was covered up with the silk sarong. "It'll only take me a few minutes to shower and pack. I could be down there in half an hour."

Amalia shook her head. "Sorry, it takes me a bit longer. I'll need the hour." She blew a kiss as she left the room.

Just like a femme, Paige thought as she got out of bed and headed for the shower. She was done in five minutes flat, and took another fifteen to dress and pack. She went down and checked out, and then killed time in the little souvenir shop. She was kind of disappointed at the tackiness of most of the items, but she ended up buying a book about the fire goddess, Pele. She checked the lobby and saw Amalia at the desk.

She approached and made a big show of looking at her watch. "When you say you need an hour, you really mean it. I've been down here for forty-five minutes."

Amalia gave her a look. "Typical butch."

With a pleased grin, Paige ignored her comment. "You want to have breakfast here, or head out?"

"Let's eat here. By the way, how are we going to manage this? I do have my own car."

"Guess you'll just have to follow me. I don't suppose you'd be interested in dropping yours off at the airport in Hilo?"

They walked to the restaurant. "Then what will I do when I get back to Kailua?"

"We'll stop at the airport there and get you another one."

The waitress seated them by the window. It gave them the opportunity to admire once again the outline of Halema'uma'u Crater in the distance. The sky was a little overcast. Clouds seemed to hover over the crater like some alien spacecraft.

"It is kind of stupid to be in two cars," Amalia said, looking at Paige over the top of her menu. "But I guess it depends on how you want to go back."

"Well, I thought we'd take the northern route. You said you wanted to see Akaka Falls. We could also be adventurous and take Saddle Road instead."

"Then we definitely have to return my car. The rental agent specifically told me I couldn't take it on Saddle Road. It could void out my rental agreement."

Paige knew full well that driving on the supposedly dangerous Saddle Road could void her rental agreement as well, but she didn't let on. "I hear it's a rough road, but my Subaru can handle it. If you want to see the observatory on Mauna Kea, it's the only way to go."

The waitress came over and took their orders. Paige couldn't help but notice the woman's tight ass as she walked away. When she glanced up, Amalia was giving her that look. Unperturbed, she said, "Can't help but notice an attractive woman."

"You're quite a flirt."

Paige grinned. "I've been called worse, but yes, you could say that. I've just never met a woman that I wanted to settle down with." She took Amalia's hand. "Of course, there's always a first time."

Amalia blushed and lowered her pretty blue eyes. "I think I'd like to take Saddle Road. We'll drop my car at the airport and reserve another one for when we get back to Kailua." She looked up at Paige again.

The waitress came with their food. Paige had decided to try the LocoMoco — a local dish consisting of a beef patty with gravy and two eggs over rice and macaroni salad. Amalia had chosen a Hawaiian fruit boat made of half a pineapple and filled with tropical fruit and lime sherbet.

Amalia took a bite of golden-orange papaya. "This has to be what Eve tempted Adam with in the Garden of Eden. Apples just don't cut it."

They finished breakfast quickly, and Amalia followed Paige to the Hilo airport to turn in her rented sedan. They traveled through the city to Kaumana Drive, which then turned into the infamous Saddle Road. The car rental agent had told them that the problem was not so much the rough road as it was the lack of gas stations and facilities. Breaking down or running out of gas on Saddle Road would incur extremely high towing expenses, ones that the rental car companies weren't willing to pay. The road also passed through a large military training base, and they could very well end up stuck behind a slow-moving convoy. With a full tank of gas and a quickly bought picnic basket of goodies, Paige confidently turned her Subaru Outback onto Saddle Road.

Driving along the curvy two-lane road, not meeting any other cars, was almost like being in another world. They passed through a verdant forest of *Ohia lehua* trees and *Hapu li* ferns, sometimes so dense it blocked out the sun and made things feel a little spooky. A sudden rain shower made the lush, earthy smells of the rain forest even stronger. The redolent scents wafted into the car, making Paige's nose twitch.

The road itself was tight — no shoulder, rough, with hills and sharp curves. Paige had to concentrate. It was also hard to get a radio station to come in, so she finally turned the radio off.

"I can't believe how beautiful this island is," Amalia commented as she looked out the rain-streaked window. "And the weird thing is, I feel like I'm in a foreign country, but I have to remind myself that this is the United States."

"I know what you mean. It's nice, though, not having to worry about changing money or speaking the language. Food is familiar, yet you can still get local dishes."

"I want to go to a luau. There's supposed to be a really excellent one at the Kona Village Resort."

"Yeah, the thought of roasted pig makes my mouth water." She glanced over at Amalia. "You're not a vegetarian or anything like that, are you?"

Amalia laughed. The sound made Paige feel awfully happy. "I try to limit my meat intake and I'm not too keen on pork, but I have to at least try it. How can you go to a luau and not? Have you eaten poi?"

"I tried it in Honolulu. Can't say I liked it much. Poi has the consistency of thick pancake batter and tastes a little bitter." She grinned. "It was kinda fun licking it off my fingers, though."

She chuckled as she watched the slow blush spread over Amalia's smooth cheeks. Amalia shyly lowered her lashes, but Paige detected a faint smile.

Amalia took a deep breath. "So, tell me more about your family. Sisters and brothers?"

Still enjoying Amalia's reaction, Paige answered, "One brother. He lives in Las Vegas. Manages a casino or something like that." She shrugged. "We don't get along much these days. Michael disapproves of my 'lifestyle.' "

"What about your parents?"

"Well, they know, but we don't discuss it. That's okay, though. Your sex life isn't something you talk about with your parents, even if you're straight."

"But being gay is more than just sex. Aren't they interested in who you're seeing? If you're happy?"

"Well, of course they are. I tell them what I want them to know. They're proud of me for getting a master's and going for a Ph.D. Neither of them went to college."

"Do you feel like telling me about your best friend's mom?"

Paige felt a twinge of anger. Her animosity wasn't directed at Amalia, but the memory of Mrs. Anderson still brought old feelings to the surface, no matter that the whole sordid affair happened nearly ten years ago. She swallowed. She just wasn't ready yet. "I'm sorry, I can't."

"That's okay."

With a soft sigh, Amalia leaned back into the seat.

Paige liked the way her hair flew around in the wind. Her profile revealed incredibly long eyelashes, a cute straight nose, full lips, and a pert little chin. When she smiled, she had dimples. Her neck was long, like a dancer's. Paige's gaze traveled along her collarbone and then lower to follow the curve of breasts just the right size, not too big and not too small.

"Watch out!"

Paige looked back at the road and swerved to avoid a mongoose. The ubiquitous little weasel-like animals had been introduced by sugar cane farmers in an attempt to control the rat population. Unfortunately, rats were nocturnal and mongooses were not. According to Mitch, they hadn't taken care of the rats, but they did wreak havoc on the native bird population and continued to do so. Paige didn't think one more dead mongoose would matter, but Amalia seemed to care, so she wasn't about to harm one if she could help it.

"You really should keep your eyes on the road," Amalia scolded, but she smiled when she looked at Paige.

"I just think you're very pretty."

She blushed. "Thank you. It's been a long time since someone's said that to me." She placed her hand lightly on Paige's bare thigh.

Her touch was warm and suggestive. Paige wanted to pull the car over and propose a quickie, but somehow she knew that would not go over well. It certainly felt strange to control her sexual impulses and become more courtly, for want of a better word. She really wasn't used to thinking about someone else's feelings. In that respect, she *was* selfish, as more than one woman had told her in the past. She didn't want Amalia to think so.

"You about ready for lunch?" she asked instead.

They'd long since left the forest and now traveled through countryside that was becoming increasingly more ranchlike. It was totally dry too; no rain showers had fallen here. They could see the slopes of Mauna Kea and its snowcapped peak. They'd encountered maybe five cars during the two-hour drive, most heading in the opposite direction. And it was rare to see any kind of buildings, giving the illusion of being completely uninhabited.

"Guess there's no sense looking for a rest stop," Amalia said.

"Don't think so. Need a potty break? You'll just have to go in the bushes."

"No need to smirk like that, Miss Parker. I've done my share of crouching."

Paige pulled over as soon as she had enough of a shoulder to do so. They ate their lunch in the car, then decided to get out for a short walk. A plain wire fence separated them from range land. The grasses were tall and golden; bits of green dotted the landscape. The air was quiet and still. Paige suddenly grabbed Amalia's arm and pointed. A short distance ahead, on the wire fence, rested a small Hawaiian owl. The creature rotated its head and looked at the two women before gracefully flying off.

"I wish I'd had my camera out," Amalia whispered. "I've got a great telephoto lens."

"You know," Paige said as she took Amalia's hand and headed back to the car, "if you like birdwatching, I've read about a wildlife refuge on the slopes of

Mauna Kea called the Hakalau Forest. It's supposed to have several species of rare birds, some on the endangered list."

Amalia clambered back into the car and waited for Paige to get in before she answered. "A couple of my friends are into birdwatching, but I've never really done it. It seems like such a nerdy pastime."

Paige could only laugh in reply.

"There's so much to see on this island," Amalia continued. "I don't know what I'd do if I was only here for a short time."

Paige started the car and headed out once again. "Do you know yet where you want to live?"

Amalia shook her head. "I figured I'd explore for a bit and then settle down in the place I like best."

"My host is a real estate agent. I'm sure he can help you out."

"I'll talk to him about it." Amalia sighed and leaned back into her seat. "Kathy would never have been able to live here. She was too much of a city girl. I had to do some fancy talking to get her to agree to buy the house where we did, but we couldn't have afforded one closer to D.C."

"What did she do?"

"We both worked for the same local television station. I was a production assistant, and Kathy was a substitute news anchor on the weekends. The jobs sound more glamorous than they paid."

Paige knew what it was like to have to watch every penny. She was dying to ask how Amalia could afford to give up her job and move to Hawaii, but she figured it would be pretty crass. Amalia had mentioned before that the insurance settlement had paid well. Could it have paid that well?

As if reading her thoughts, Amalia volunteered, "In addition to the insurance settlements, Kathy had also taken out life and mortgage insurance. I felt I needed a permanent change of scene, so here I am." She smiled at Paige. "It's about as far away from Maryland as I can get and still be in the States."

Paige took her hand and kissed it gently. "I'm really sorry about what happened. I know you're probably tired of hearing that, but it's true."

"Thank you."

They fell into a comfortable silence. Despite the heat, they drove with the windows open. It was almost eerily quiet without the traffic noise or sirens or trains or anything else one normally encountered on the road. The rolling landscape unfurled all around them, punctuated with tall hills and little mountains in softly rounded shapes that dipped and crested like women's bodies. Paige suddenly stopped the car and pointed. There, on a sign, was the warning: "Beware of Artillery Shells Overhead."

"Oh, my God," Amalia exclaimed, "do you think it's safe to drive through?"

Paige felt an adrenaline surge. "Mitch told me about this, but he said it's safe." She started the car. "Let's hope he's right."

They passed through the military training ground without incident. They didn't even encounter a convoy. Paige was disappointed that they saw no artillery shells. She was sure Amalia would be frightened, and she would have welcomed the opportunity to hold and comfort her.

A while later, Paige glanced over and saw that Amalia had fallen asleep with her head against the partially rolled-up window. Even in sleep, she looked exhausted. The circles under her eyes were dark against her pale skin. Her mouth was open, her breathing deep and steady. Pale reddish-blonde hair fell softly against her cheek and neck.

As Paige turned left off of Saddle Road and onto Mamalahoa Highway, she knew she wanted to get to know this woman. And that for the first time in her life, she'd met someone who really mattered. But could she trust her?

Chapter Nine

Back at Brent and Scot's B&B, Amalia slept well and woke early the next day. She'd been tempted to ask Paige to spend the night, but her exhaustion was just too great. She stretched and decided that today she'd take it easy. After all, she was going to be living here from now on. There was no need to try and squeeze everything in all at once as if she were on some two-week vacation.

She thought about all she'd seen in the last three days. She felt her face flush as she remembered what had happened Wednesday night. She'd never slept with someone that quickly. Still, she had to admit it had felt wonderful to touch a woman again and to be touched in return. She traced the scar on her chest and belly. She'd wondered if she'd ever feel attractive again, but Paige had certainly made it clear that she was. She closed her eyes and ran her fingers lightly across her lips, reliving Paige's kisses. Just the thought of her, so much like Kathy and yet so different, made her tremble inside.

She glanced at Kathy's photo on the nightstand and then, with a deep sigh, threw the covers off and got out of bed. After a quick, hot shower, she was dressed and drinking coffee in Scot and Brent's living room. They'd left her a note along with breakfast. Scot had chosen to fly to Oahu with Brent and they would be spending the night. She thought it a bit odd at first that they would leave a guest alone, but she was glad they were comfortable enough with her to do so. Maybe she'd ask Paige to stay with her. They were to meet tonight to go on a manta ray dive.

She got up from the couch and dialed the number Paige had given her. A man answered and she asked for Paige. A moment later, Paige's voice made goose bumps rise on Amalia's arms.

"You want to spend the day together?" Amalia asked, suddenly feeling spontaneous. "I thought we might drive up to the Parker Ranch in Waimea." So much for her decision to take it easy.

"You just don't know when to stop, do you? I think you need to rest before our dive tonight."

Amalia felt a flash of irritation even though Paige's tone had been teasing. She'd had people telling her these past two years what she should do, and she wasn't about to let some stranger do it now.

"I think I know what I need," she said, hearing the anger in her voice.

"I'm just trying to watch out for you, Amalia. Why don't we go to the beach? Get some sun. Maybe swim a little to get used to the water for tonight."

Amalia knew lazing around on the sand would still be resting, but she decided Paige did have a point. She really had overdone it this last week or so. And she did owe Paige for having cut short the hike.

"Sorry I was so curt. The beach sounds great. There's lots of smaller ones around here. Which one were you thinking of?"

"Hold on a sec." Amalia heard murmuring voices, then Paige came back. "Actually, Mitch just offered to take us snorkeling. You think you could drive here and meet us?"

"Well, there's only one problem. I don't have a car anymore, remember? We forgot to stop at the airport and pick one up."

"Damn! Okay, I'm on the way."

Amalia hung up, feeling a little guilty. It was because she'd been sleeping that Paige had decided against stopping for a car. Well, maybe Paige would like a quick soak in the hot tub. It would be about thirty minutes or so before she arrived, and Amalia decided to make the most of it.

She jumped back into the shower to wet her skin, then smoothed scented lotion all over her body. She put on the blue-and-gold swimsuit and a sheer cover-up, which she buttoned up to the neck. In the mirror, she examined herself. Still too thin, but she was beginning to fill out. At least she didn't look so bony anymore. She brushed her hair until it gleamed and used a curling iron to make it flip slightly at the ends.

It was past her shoulders now, longer than it had been in years. She applied a touch of mascara, some blush, and pink lip gloss. She smiled and shook her head at her foolishness. If Paige accepted her offer to play in the hot tub, her makeup wouldn't last long. Ditto if she went snorkeling.

She heard Paige's car drive up and went outside to meet her. Paige's indrawn breath made Amalia laugh. Actually, she was impressed with Paige too. Her tight bicycle shorts showed off her muscular, tanned legs to perfection, and a white tank top exposed equally muscular arms. No doubt about it, this woman was hot. She probably had women falling all over themselves to get into her bed.

"Maybe we should stay here," Paige said as she took Amalia into her arms and kissed her deeply.

Amalia's body reacted swiftly. Almost dizzy with lust, she took Paige's hand and placed it between her legs. She wrapped her arms around Paige's neck and grabbed hold of her hair. Paige growled in response and kissed Amalia's neck. Amalia bit Paige's shoulder. Paige clutched the see-through cover-up, and then the sound of fabric ripping made Amalia's breath catch in her throat as the flimsy material floated down around her ankles.

In one movement, Paige picked her up and carried her into the house. She found Amalia's bedroom somehow and placed her none too gently on the bed. The swimsuit came off, and then Paige's mouth and hands were all over her. She almost felt like she was being devoured. Frantically, she grabbed Paige's hand and pushed it down, down between her legs where she ached with wanting. She gasped and arched up as Paige's long fingers found their mark.

She lost herself in the sensation of being filled. Paige thrust hard and deep until Amalia could wait no longer. "I want your mouth," she moaned.

Paige pulled her fingers away, leaving Amalia feeling temporarily empty. Then her mouth was there, hot and urgent with desire. It didn't take long before her body trembled with release. She called out Paige's name as the strength drained from her, leaving her helpless. Collapsed against the pillows that had somehow wound up under her, she sighed. When Paige made love to her, it left her pleasantly weak until she got that surge of energy.

The surge came, and she kissed Paige as she quickly removed the bicycle shorts and tank top. Her hands traveled over that wondrous body, and she felt a thrill of satisfaction as Paige responded to her touch. The minutes melted into hours as they made love again and again. It was well past noon when they finally rested in each other's arms.

"Do you want to try the hot tub?" Amalia asked softly, nuzzling Paige's neck.

"Mmmm, sounds good, but I think Mitch is probably already wondering where we are. I suppose I should at least call him."

Amalia sat up. "I'm dying of thirst." Paige was stretched out in all her naked glory. Amalia leaned over and kissed her breast, taking a nipple into her mouth.

"You start that and we'll never get out of bed," Paige said, laughing as she pushed Amalia away.

"Well, okay," Amalia conceded. She smiled wickedly and ran her nails over Paige's sensitive stomach. Just as Paige reached for her, she leaped out of bed.

"Witch!"

"C'mon, sexy, let's go look at tropical fish."

Amalia put her swimsuit back on but didn't bother with the torn cover-up. She grabbed shorts and a T-shirt and then bounced out of the bedroom and to the kitchen, leaving Paige to follow at a more leisurely pace.

After a shared glass of iced tea and some macaroons, they made a quick trip to the airport to pick up another car for Amalia. This time she splurged and rented a white Le Baron convertible. She was feeling much more free and easy. A sedan was so stuffy. She was young, she was rich, and she was with a most exciting woman. She was sure that Paige had a sexual bag of tricks, most of which she hadn't even seen yet. As she followed the Subaru down Kuakini Highway, she let her fantasies run wild. She almost felt nineteen again.

Paige was impressed when Amalia rented the convertible. She was tempted to leave her own car parked at the airport so she could ride with her. She kept glancing into the rearview mirror, wondering at the secretive smile on Amalia's face. The woman had turned out to be quite a surprise — passionate and eager. She was sure there was a sexual side to her that Amalia wasn't even aware of, and if Paige had anything to say about it, she'd help Amalia discover it.

The drive to Captain Cook seemed to take no time at all. She was glad to see Mitch's Jeep Cherokee. It meant he hadn't gotten a call to take a client out house-hunting. She got out of the car and watched Amalia step carefully down the steep driveway.

"I parked up there," Amalia said. "That driveway is too steep. I was afraid to drive down 'cause it felt like my car would just tip over."

Paige laughed. "Yeah, it is pretty scary." She took Amalia's hand. "Let's go get Mitch."

Just then Mitch came down the stairs. "You must be Amalia," he said, taking her hand. "You're as pretty as Paige said."

Amalia blushed. "Thanks."

He gestured toward the snorkeling gear hanging from the lattice wall. "You'll need a mask and flippers. Just try these on until you find some that are comfortable. The mask needs to be airtight so water doesn't get in."

When they finally had their equipment picked out, they piled into Mitch's Jeep for the trip to the beach. It actually wasn't a beach, Paige saw. Instead of sand, there was an expanse of gray-black rock, upon which several people had spread out blankets and towels. Crevices in the rock were filled with seawater and little creatures — tiny crabs and miniature sea urchins.

They put down their towels, and Mitch pointed to his left. "That's Pu'uhonua o Honaunau over there, the Place of Refuge."

Across the expanse of clear blue water and swimming distance away, Paige could see what looked like a fort. Tall, weathered-gray wooden totems with elaborate headdresses, elongated faces, and toothy grimaces stood guard. Perched on a group of boulders that appeared to have tumbled into the water, another totem guarded the sacred site, waves licking its feet. It wasn't quite as tall and thin as the others. To Paige, the face with its oversized eye sockets reminded her of drawings of so-called space aliens.

"It is quite awe inspiring," Mitch continued. "In the ancient days, defeated warriors and those accused of breaking the *kapus*, or sacred laws, would flee to this *heiau* to be ritually purified by the priests and therefore set free. It was a chance for a new life, if they survived the dangerous journey."

"Dangerous? In what way?"

"Well, remember, they were being pursued. If caught, they would be killed. The waters were dangerous too, full of sharks."

Paige eyed the water uneasily. "Sharks?"

"You don't have to worry about them here in the inlet." He stood up and put on his mask. "Let's go, girls."

They put on their flippers, snorkels, and masks and stepped awkwardly across the rock to the edge. A small outcropping of rock provided a platform, and from there Mitch slid easily into the water. The two women followed suit. Paige gasped at the first touch of cold water, but her body soon acclimated to the temperature. The water was crystal clear, and she followed Mitch and Amalia's shimmering shapes. Down below her, dark rocks bloomed with coral and sponges and waving sea anemones. Fish in jeweled colors of yellow and purple and orange darted back and forth, seemingly so close that Paige reached out automatically.

Mitch had given her a quick lesson in snorkeling the first time she'd gone out with him. It had taken her a while to get the hang of it because besides being more used to scuba diving, she hadn't been in the ocean in quite a while. She'd swallowed plenty of saltwater the other day, but she decided to give it another try. Taking a deep breath, she plunged lower into the water, delighted when her fingers brushed against a sticky sea anemone. Mitch had warned her against touching the coral — oil from her skin was deadly to them — but after six years of school she knew that already.

She kicked to the surface again and blew water out of her snorkel. Mitch and Amalia bobbed in the water ahead. Mitch pointed at something, while Amalia gestured excitedly. Paige joined them just in time to see two giant sea turtles swim gracefully by. She was awed; this was what she had gone to school for — to help save magnificent creatures like these. She fought the temptation to try and swim closer to them. It was illegal in Hawaii to touch or harass any marine life.

The three continued swimming farther out. Though a little nervous, Paige felt comfortable knowing Mitch was there. Below them, the sea floor dipped deeper, its white sand gleaming in the shafts of sunlight. Schools of fish darted by. The rocky outcroppings held mysteries in their darkly shadowed recesses and crevices.

The turtles swam by them again, and Paige could swear one of them brushed against her. She lifted her head out of the water and saw that Mitch and Amalia had done the same. They simultaneously took off their masks and snorkels, treading water all the while.

"Was that incredible or what?" Amalia said, her blue eyes sparkling with excitement. They almost matched the vivid blue of the ocean around them.

"You two doing okay?" Mitch asked.

"Oh yes," they both replied.

"I think we should head back in. Don't want to overdo it your first time," he said, speaking to Amalia. "We'll have a bit of lunch and then swim out again."

Smiling indulgently, they put their masks and

snorkels back on and followed Mitch once again as he led them to shore. Paige turned away from the sea creatures so she could watch Amalia. She seemed to be at home in the ocean, her body gliding through the water like some sea creature itself. The undulating waves and the sun formed shadows across her sleek form. Her long hair flowed behind like golden threads. On impulse, Paige kicked harder and caught up with Amalia, grabbing her around the waist. They sputtered to the surface and laughingly took off their masks.

"You frightened me," Amalia scolded, but she had a big smile on her face.

"I just wanted to do this before we got too close to shore," Paige replied. Still holding Amalia, she kissed her. Their legs, kicking to tread water, entwined. She kissed Amalia's neck, tasting salt.

Amalia moaned, the sound coming from deep within her. Paige continued to kiss her and hold her, helped by the buoyancy of the water. Her hands slid down Amalia's hips, down her thighs and then up again to cup her ass. She squeezed gently. A Scorpio and thus a water sign, Paige had always been drawn to the sea. And now she knew that more than anything, she wanted to make love to this woman while the salty seawater washed over her body.

"Let's go back," she said reluctantly.

"You certainly know how to make a woman feel good," Amalia said. Her voice was as shaky as Paige felt.

They broke apart and put on their masks and snorkels once again. Mitch was already almost to shore. They kicked hard to catch up with him. He waited for them in the water. As they approached, he pointed to the underwater rocks. There, in one of the

110

crevices, a moray eel with its sinister-looking face almost blended right into the shadows. The sight made a shiver go up Paige's spine. With a grin, Mitch swam away and they followed, using the waves to help float them back to the rock platform.

Chapter Ten

They spent the rest of the afternoon lounging on the rocks and taking short snorkeling trips. They didn't want to get too tired for the manta ray dive later that night. Thanking Mitch profusely, they drove in separate cars directly from his house to the marina near the Kona Surf Resort and Country Club. A small boat named the *Sea Princess* and its crew of three awaited them in the parking lot.

"You'll need to wear these wetsuits," the captain said as he handed Amalia and Paige each a suit.

The four others going on the dive, a husband and

wife with two daughters, wore their own wetsuits. Although scuba certified, Paige had chosen to snorkel with Amalia. The wife and the younger daughter would also be snorkeling, but the dad and oldest daughter would be scuba diving. Amalia couldn't help but laugh as she wriggled into the tight rubber suit and watched Paige do the same.

"I can't breathe in this thing," Paige complained.

"You need it to maintain your body temperature," the captain replied with a toothy grin. "You'll be amazed at how cold the water can get at night."

"It's very flattering," Amalia added as she eyed Paige's muscular form in the snug hot-pink rubber. Her own suit was a bright lemon yellow. The suits covered their torsos, thighs, and upper arms.

"Yeah, I'll bet," Paige retorted, but Amalia could tell she was pleased.

The captain gathered everyone around. "This is my wife, Julia. She'll help you with whatever you need." He smiled. "And she'll serve hot chocolate and cookies on the way back." He pointed to another man. "This is Robert. He'll be videotaping our dive."

Robert stepped forward. "I'll be taping the whole time. I've been on these dives several times. I try to be sure to capture everyone in the video." He grinned at each of them in turn. "After the dive, you'll be able to preview the video and hopefully will decide to purchase a copy."

The captain continued. "You two divers will go with me to the bottom of the ocean floor. We'll stay there near the rocks and coral. The lights on the ocean floor attract the plankton that the rays feed on, and so the rays will pass very close. You snorkelers will stay mostly on the surface, but you'll see the rays just as well. These flashlights will attract them to you."

"Just how big are these things?" one of the girls asked.

"They have wingspans of fourteen feet," Paige said automatically, "but they're very gentle. No need to be afraid."

The captain looked at her in surprise. "You've done this before?"

"I'm a marine biologist."

"Really? That's so exciting," the girl exclaimed. Her eyes shone with admiration.

The captain spoke. "We'll be staying out about an hour. Okay. Are we ready?"

Once the *Sea Princess* was in the water, they all clambered aboard. The girl sat next to Paige and plied her with questions. Amalia couldn't help but smile at the sight, but night was falling quickly, and the ever-darkening water made her nervous. It was just choppy enough to make the boat rock sickeningly back and forth. Amalia was glad they'd both taken Dramamine beforehand, although Paige had insisted she didn't need it. In only a matter of minutes, the captain dropped anchor. Darkness surrounded them — black sky, black water — and even the moon remained hidden. A chill wind swept in off the ocean, raising goose bumps on Amalia's skin. She could feel her nipples harden inside the tight wetsuit.

Other boats were anchored nearby. They all formed a sort of wide semicircle around a patch of glowing blue-green light. Amalia could barely make out the forms of other swimmers as she watched the bobbing lights shining from the tips of their snorkels. It seemed that each boat used a different color so that the crews could locate their own clients. Their color was green.

They all put on their flippers and masks. The family of four all jumped confidently into the water, followed by Paige. Amalia hesitated on the edge, adjusting her mask yet again. The water was so incredibly dark. Terror flashed inside her, then she took a deep breath and plunged in.

The shock of the cold water made her involuntarily open her mouth. She gulped saltwater and came gasping to the surface. She almost screamed when something brushed her arm, but then she realized it was Paige.

"Oh, Jesus, Paige," she breathed, "you scared me to death."

"Sorry, sweetie." She touched Amalia's arm again. "Are you going to be okay?"

"Yes. I just got panicky for a second. Let's go."

She put on her snorkel and dipped her head in the water before she could change her mind. Her body seemed to be adjusting quickly to the temperature. She snapped on her flashlight and followed Paige's form toward the blue-green light. The plankton looked like hundreds of snowflakes. Suddenly, an enormous creature emerged from the darkness and into the light. It swooped gracefully in a large circle, showing first a white belly and then its black-gray back, its wings like a butterfly in flight. Its gills were open, forming a wide mouth. Amalia could see inside its body, see what appeared to be a big rib cage. *It's harmless,* she told herself, but she frantically kicked away as the ray swam nearer. It turned again, making another circle, scooping and filtering plankton through its gills. Then it disappeared down into the darkness.

Amalia turned, looking for Paige. She was reassuringly close. Amalia trained her flashlight toward the ocean bottom once again, seeing the forms of several rays as they circled like gymnasts in a tumbling routine. Several fish also passed into the light. Paige touched her arm and pointed out three big red ones.

The people with scuba gear seemed far away. Amalia saw who she thought was the father in their group duck his head as a ray swam close by. She noticed Robert, the videographer, with his powerful light. The brightness seemed to attract the rays. Several fellow snorkelers floated on the ocean surface. Sound was muffled. The water remained choppy, making Amalia a bit queasy. She suddenly felt incredibly cold; her teeth were chattering. The wetsuit afforded little protection after all. She lifted her head from the water, wondering how much time was left to their dive. As fascinating as it was, she wanted it to be over. Paige was beside her again.

"Aren't they the most amazing sight? So beautiful."

"I know it's silly, but they're a little scary too."

"They can't hurt you."

"Yes, I know. Say, do you have any idea how long we've been out here? I'm terribly cold."

"I'd say about an hour. You want to go back to the boat? I'll come with you."

Amalia glanced over at the rocking boat. "I think I'd get sick if I got up on it."

"Let's head on over anyway."

They swam to the boat. Amalia clung to the ladder, wanting to get onboard and yet not. She smiled as she watched Paige float around, shining her flashlight. She looked into the water and saw several rays under the boat. Paige obviously saw them too, for she dove several times to get nearer. It seemed to Amalia that Paige could hold her breath an awfully long time.

Finally, the rest of their group appeared and climbed into the boat one by one. Shivering, Amalia gratefully stripped off her wetsuit and wrapped a warm towel around her body. The two daughters spoke animatedly about what they'd seen, Paige's admirer once again sitting close. Julia passed around hot chocolate and cookies as they motored back to the marina. On land once more, Amalia and Paige headed for the public restrooms to change into dry clothing, but the others gathered round a picnic table for a preview of Robert's video.

Inside the restroom, Paige pushed Amalia against the wall. "Need help changing out of that wet bathing suit?" she asked, kissing Amalia's sensitive neck.

Amalia felt an immediate reaction to Paige's touch. A thrill ran through her at the thought of getting caught. With a glance at the door, she whispered, "Yes, help me."

Paige stripped off the swimsuit, her hands rough, her mouth hot against Amalia's chilled skin. Amalia kissed her, tasting salt. The gritty cement wall bit into Amalia's back, but she didn't care. All she felt was Paige's mouth and fingers as they blazed a fire across her skin. She pulled Paige to her, urging her ever downward. Paige knelt on the floor, holding tight to Amalia's ass as her tongue teased her clit.

Amalia gasped, struggling to brace herself against the wall. She held Paige's head. Her legs trembled; her knees grew weak. It seemed like only seconds had passed when she felt the orgasm build like fire in her veins before she came in an explosion of bright lights and orange-gold flame.

She muffled her cries with her fists as her knees finally gave out and she sank to the cement floor, taking Paige with her. Paige laughed softly and stroked her hair.

"You are so hot," Paige whispered. "And quick!"

"I can't believe that just happened." Amalia glanced at the doorway. "Do you think they heard us?"

Paige laughed again, a full-throated sound that made Amalia shiver. Then she stood and held out her hand. Amalia let her pull her up. She could see under the bright light how her scars stood out whitely against the pink blush of her skin. Unexpectedly, tears welled up in her eyes, and she quickly grabbed a towel to cover her body. Despite the incredible experience of what had just happened, she suddenly felt unattractive and unworthy.

Paige gently took the towel from her. She kissed Amalia's body everywhere the scars crisscrossed. "You are so beautiful," she told Amalia between kisses. "And these scars are your badge of courage. Don't ever be ashamed by them."

The tears flowed freely then. It was as if making love this time had released all those emotions that she kept tightly in check, at least in front of others. She missed Kathy intensely at that moment, almost feeling guilty, as if she had betrayed her somehow. Paige kissed her tears away and held her close.

"Just let it all out, sweetheart," she soothed. Her touch, which only moments before had been rough and purposeful, now calmed and comforted.

After a few minutes, Amalia sniffed once and

pushed away. She dried her eyes with the towel. "I don't know what came over me."

Paige handed Amalia her clothes. "I'm no psychologist, but I think you're finally letting go of all the stress you've been under." She grinned. "Sex can be just what the doctor ordered."

Amalia answered with a grin of her own. "Well, you're right about that. I never thought I'd feel this way again."

They exited the bathroom and were surprised to discover Robert still waiting for them. The others appeared to have left. He gave them a lecherous grin. Hotly embarrassed, Amalia felt her face flush. Paige was unfazed.

"My friend suffered a bit of seasickness," she explained. "How much is the video?"

Hating the way his eyes looked her over, Amalia headed toward the car. She felt torn between wanting a permanent reminder of their dive with the manta rays and wanting to deny him a dime. Paige soon joined her.

"Did you order a video?" Amalia asked.

"Yup. He'll deliver it to Mitch's tomorrow." She winked. "Won't he be surprised to find a man at the house?"

"It makes me uncomfortable that he knows where you're staying."

"I'm a big girl. I can take care of myself. I really don't think we have anything to worry about from ol' Robert." She opened the car door. "I'm starved. Where do you want to go for dinner?"

"There's this great little Mexican place over on Alii Drive. Nice view of the ocean from the balcony — if you get the right table."

"Mexican it is."

At the restaurant, they had to wait a bit for a table out on the balcony. A building blocked their view of the ocean, but it was too dark to see it anyway. Amalia felt relaxed but still a bit embarrassed by her reaction after they'd made love. Well, "had sex" would be more accurate, she supposed. And it certainly had been one-sided.

Sipping her margarita, she looked across the table at Paige reading over the menu. In the flickering candlelight, her skin glowed the color of dark honey. Her hair, curling ever so slightly, was beginning to lighten to a softer blonde from the sun. Hard to believe they'd only known each other three days, Amalia mused. Well, four if you counted Tuesday night.

She certainly had no illusions about being in love or any of that nonsense. Alexander would scold her if she even hinted at such a thing. That reminded her, she needed to call him tonight. She looked at her watch; it was almost eleven. That meant it was only six o'clock back home in Maryland. On a Friday night, Alexander would be heading over to J. R.'s, but not until late.

"You know what you want yet?"

Paige's question interrupted her thoughts. She smiled. "I think I'll just get the cheese enchiladas with ranchero sauce. I still feel a bit queasy from that boat ride."

"Mmmm, I'm starving so it's the San Antonio platter for me." She folded up her menu. "Thanks for telling me about the dive. It was fascinating."

The waitress came over and took their orders. Amalia dipped a nacho chip into salsa and took a bite.

"You must do things like that all the time, being a marine biologist and all."

Paige sighed. "Not really. I've spent most of my time on land, in school." She laughed. "I got my scuba certification in a swimming pool."

"What will you do now?"

"Well, I'll get my Ph.D. from the university here and then maybe join a research team. The university's doing some amazing studies on the chambered nautilus. And I know that McSweeney fellow is doing really innovative work with whales here."

"What about teaching?"

Paige shook her head. "I studied marine biology so I could make a difference. Maybe become another Jacques Cousteau. I don't want to spend my life in some stuffy classroom."

Amalia reached over and took Paige's hand. "I'm sure you'll make a difference, no matter what you decide."

Paige kissed Amalia's hand. "I hope so. I certainly hope so."

Amalia trembled at the burning desire she saw reflected in Paige's dark brown eyes. If she wasn't careful, this woman could become very important in her life. Too important. She wasn't looking for anything permanent. She released Paige's hand and picked up her margarita. At least, not yet.

Chapter Eleven

Paige drove slowly back to Mitch's after dinner. She was disappointed that Amalia had refused to spend the night with her. She hadn't even wanted to take a walk along the stretch of beach on Kailua Bay. They'd parted with a vague "I'll call you" from Amalia. Paige frowned. She'd used that very line herself several times. And of course she hadn't called the woman in question.

Was it only her imagination that they'd had an incredible three days together? Hell, it was better than incredible. It was also uncharacteristic of her. She didn't usually see someone again after a casual pickup. She smiled. Well, there was no way Amalia was a casual pickup. Who did she think she was fooling?

Blinking in the bright glare of someone's high beams, she thought briefly of Marianne. They'd been lovers an entire semester, and Paige had even remained faithful. But if she was honest with herself, she'd admit her loyalty stemmed more from lack of time than any conscious decision. Marianne had been a convenient diversion from the intense study during those final weeks.

She was beginning to see a side of herself that she didn't really like. She'd treated women as mere play-things. How was that different from how men treated them? But she'd never been deliberately cruel and she was, if she said so herself, a good lover. Always considerate of their needs and desires over her own. And her account at the local florist was always high.

She knew she still had a lot of issues with trust. And she realized Rory was right, it did stem from the affair with Mrs. Anderson. The woman had seduced a sixteen-year old girl, and when she tired of her, had forbidden her daughter to associate with Paige anymore. She'd even gone to Paige's parents and com-plained about Paige's "unnatural" feelings for her daughter, little caring that they were only friends. That betrayal, coming so soon on the heels of Aunt Maggie's departure, had left behind an angry child who didn't care who she hurt. And it hadn't helped that her own parents wouldn't believe her.

Still, she was no longer a fresh-faced teenager. At twenty-four, it was time for her to get beyond all that and think seriously about her future — one that included finding a woman with whom she wanted to spend her life. And that woman could very well be Amalia.

She felt a protectiveness toward her, but whether it stemmed from sympathy over what Amalia had suffered or from something else, she didn't know. All she knew was that in a short time, Amalia had stirred her heart, and she didn't want to lose her.

Turning at the Internet Café, she drove the last leg to Mitch's. As late as it was, the lights were on in the house. She hoped he wouldn't still be up because she really didn't feel like answering any questions or making small talk. What she really wanted to do was call Rory. If anyone could help her sort this out, he could.

Mitch had indeed gone to bed. She looked at the clock. It was almost two in the morning. Only nine on the East Coast. Rory didn't go out much anymore, and even if he did, it was too early. She never could figure out why most gay men seemed to think eleven was the witching hour. After getting a glass of pineapple juice from the kitchen, she settled into Mitch's big soft chair and dialed the phone.

"Hi, Rory," she said as soon as he picked up. "It's Paige."

"Girl! Where have you been? I expected daily updates from you, and I haven't heard from you at all."

"I've just been real busy. Trying to see as much of Hawaii as possible."

"I haven't gotten a postcard yet either," he scolded.

"You will. I sent one either Tuesday or Wednesday."

He coughed suddenly. She didn't like the sound of

it, but she said nothing. He hated it when she did. "So, have you picked up many Hawaiian girls?"

She laughed. "Not Hawaiian, no. Actually, I've been good."

"That's what all the girls say. Or so I've been told. Now, don't tell me the Paige Parker I know has gone celibate?"

"I didn't say that, Rory. But I have met someone who's pretty special." He coughed again. This time she asked, "Are you okay? I don't like the sound of that cough."

"Just a little setback. Nothing to worry about. And yes, before you nag, I did go see the doctor. He's got me on antibiotics. Enough about me. Who is she?"

Paige smiled as the image of Amalia came to mind. "She's a blonde with blue eyes. Tall. And older than me."

"Name?" he prompted.

"Amalia Grant. She's really nice. I met her at the volcano."

"Did you sleep with her?" Rory asked with characteristic bluntness.

"You know me."

He laughed and then dissolved into a fit of coughing. She waited patiently. "Well," he said, "I hope you were safe."

She felt a twinge of guilt. That reminded her, she'd promised Amalia to get tested. She made a mental note to ask Mitch if this island had a clinic. "She's been celibate for two years and monogamous before that. You certainly know how to put a damper on things, don't you?"

"Are you sure you can believe her? No bisexual surprises like Marianne?"

"Yes, I believe her. Her lover was killed in a horrible car accident two years ago and Amalia was terribly injured. She's been in physical therapy all this time."

"I just worry about you. You're a little wild with the ladies. By the way, Marianne came by here. She was surprised to see me. Guess she didn't believe you really were leaving."

"What's she still doing in Dartmouth? She was supposed to go home for the summer."

"Seems she's living with some guy named Richard."

Feeling her blood pressure begin to rise, she changed the subject quickly. "Did you find a new place yet?"

There was a long pause. "I . . . I've decided to move back home."

Paige was taken aback. Home? Rory had left home over eight years ago when his parents found out he was gay. He'd told her that they said he was dead in their eyes. As far as she knew, he'd had no contact with them since.

"Home? Like back-to-your-parents home?"

"Soon after you left, I called them. They were really happy to hear from me. I was so surprised. I told them I was sick. Mom was wonderful. She told me to come home. That she didn't want me dying alone."

His words sent a chill through her. He was obviously more ill than he'd let on. She suddenly knew she might never see Rory again, and she felt her throat grow tight. "I'm glad for you," was all she could say.

"I really appreciate everything you did for me. I'll

be leaving the apartment before the end of the month. Next week, in fact. I'm sorry you paid all that rent for nothing. Mom and Dad are driving up to get me. That old VW of yours finally died."

"Don't worry about the apartment. And take anything you want."

"You take care, darlin'. I love you."

"I love you too."

Paige suddenly felt very tired, and when she turned out the light and went to bed, she did something she hadn't done in years. She cried.

On Saturday morning, the aroma of fresh coffee woke Amalia early. After her late night, she'd been sure she'd sleep until at least noon, but a glance at the clock told her it was only seven. Tempted to turn over and go back to sleep, she decided to get up. She shared her shower with several geckos, who seemed to like the steam as it rose to the ceiling.

Remembering that Scot and Brent weren't supposed to be back from Oahu until later that morning, Amalia peered cautiously into the living room. Either they'd set the coffee maker on automatic or someone else was in the house. The latter proved to be true. A young Hawaiian woman puttered around the kitchen. In contrast to the plain gray sweats she wore, she had tucked a brilliant red hibiscus into her long dark hair. When she took fresh-baked muffins out of the oven, Amalia's mouth watered.

"Excuse me," Amalia said.

The woman turned around and smiled. "*Aloha.* Good morning, Amalia. I am Leilani. I occasionally help out Scot and Brent when they need to be out of town."

She was, Amalia decided, breathtakingly beautiful. She could be one of the hula dancers in Kim Taylor Reece's photos. Nonplussed, Amalia poured herself a cup of coffee. "They didn't say anything about that. Just left me a note saying they wouldn't be around this morning."

Leilani tipped the muffins out of their pan. "I'm not surprised," she said. "They often forget to tell their guests about me. One day someone will shoot me."

"I certainly hope not!"

Leilani laughed. "Me too. Now, they told me you like your coffee black and poppyseed muffins." She opened the refrigerator. "I also cut up some papaya and mangoes."

"This is very nice. Thank you. *Mahalo*." Amalia stood at the counter and took a bite of juicy papaya, squeezing lemon on it first like she'd seen others do. "So, how do you know Scot and Brent?"

"Brent and my brother used to be lovers. They're not friends anymore, but I liked Brent too much to write him off."

"It must create tension between you and your brother."

"Some, but he works on Richard Chamberlain's ranch on Oahu so I don't see him much."

Amalia took a mango spear. "That must be exciting. Has he actually met him?" She'd loved Richard Chamberlain in *The Thorn Birds* miniseries.

Leilani leaned against the counter and shook her head. "He wishes," she said with a laugh.

"I'd like to do some sightseeing today. I thought I'd drive north. Any recommendations?"

"You've got to visit Pu'ukohola Heiau National Park in South Kohala. The *heiau* there is the largest one built by King Kamehameha."

"I saw that wonderful statue of him in Honolulu."

"Oh, that one is just a copy. The original bronze statue is in Kapaau." She began to wash the breakfast dishes. "It actually has quite an interesting history. The original was supposedly lost at sea and so the copy was commissioned. Soon after, the original was found in the Falkland Islands."

"I should take a class in Hawaiian history. We don't learn these kinds of things in school."

Leilani poured herself a cup of coffee and took a long sip. "You know, King Kamehameha lived out his final days right here in Kailua-Kona. Things changed much after his death."

"He was the one who united all the islands, right?"

"Yes. We commemorate the life of Kamehameha every year in June. The state holiday is Friday. On Saturday there will be a big parade starting at nine."

Amalia put her cup into the sink. "I look forward to it. *Mahalo*. See you later."

She returned to her room to grab her knapsack and windbreaker. She paused by the phone, wondering if she should call Paige. On the phone last night, Alexander had told her to cool things a bit to avoid the lesbian U-Haul syndrome. She'd laughed. After just three days she had no intention of moving in with anyone. She resolutely ignored the phone and went out to the car. In only a matter of minutes she was turning onto Queen Kaahumanu Highway and then passing the airport. Once again, she drove through the parched countryside of black and brown lava and scrub brush. She'd learned from Scot that what she thought were white rocks decorating the lava were in fact white coral. She drove slowly along one stretch of highway where the speed limit was lowered and searched the area. It was here that one might see the Kona Nightingales, a herd of wild donkeys that "sang." Brent told her she had a better chance of seeing them at night, and indeed she passed through the area with nary a glimpse of them.

She made a left onto Waikoloa Beach Drive. Almost immediately the scenery changed. Lush green surrounded her, watered by a massive irrigation system. Like other resorts, the Waikoloa Beach Resort boasted a huge eighteen-hole golf course, but it was the petroglyph field that Amalia wanted to see. She parked the car and decided to do a little shopping first. The King's Shops had all sorts of interesting boutiques and restaurants. She stopped first at a florist and bought herself a lei of fragrant plumeria. The pale Hawaiian flower with its golden starburst center was fast becoming her favorite. After buying several gifts to send back home, including a signed Kim Taylor Reece print of a male hula dancer for Alexander, she grabbed a quick bite at a Chinese restaurant. Stopping for a banana-flavored shaved ice, she then headed out to the petroglyph field. It was baking hot, and she was glad for her wide-brimmed straw hat and long-sleeved white cotton shirt that she wore open as a jacket.

The field lay in the midst of a brilliantly green golf course. Heeding the warning at the beginning, Amalia made sure to stay on the indicated path through the field. She was glad she'd worn her hiking boots because the path was rough and full of crumbling rocks. The gray-brown rock was decorated with carved petroglyphs — primitive line carvings of people and animals and symbols. Amalia walked slowly through the field, stopping occasionally to take a photo of a particularly interesting carving. Some were easily recognizable — a sea turtle and some stick figures of people. Other carvings were composed of circles and dots and swirling lines, forming some symbol or story known only to those who had carved them. She knelt down and traced one deep carving with her fingers, wondering about the person who'd formed it. Was it a man or a woman? Were they happy? To or from where were they traveling?

According to her guidebook, this particular petroglyph field had been part of a massive ancient highway. It included several natural-formed caves as well as man-made C-shaped windbreaks constructed from piles of rocks. Amalia ventured off the path to look into one of the caves where travelers used to take shelter. The opening was exactly as tall as she and very wide. Despite the heat of the day, it was cool inside, and she crouched down, trying to imagine what it had been like to camp there.

Leaving the welcome coolness of the cave, she continued to the end of the field and turned back. It seemed so incongruous to be walking through this ancient slice of history and be surrounded by a golf course. She half expected to find a golf ball or two nestled among the cracks and crevices. Nearer the shopping area, on the paved road that bordered the petroglyph field, a golf cart motored slowly along. The elderly female occupant waved to Amalia. She smiled and waved back.

At the car once more, she lowered the convertible top and headed back out onto the highway. She passed two more resort communities before turning left onto Kawaihae Road. A right would have taken her to Waimea, the bustling little town in the heart of *paniolo* country. That was a trip she'd take with Paige.

She pulled up to the white building that housed the information center for Pu'ukohola. Despite several cars outside, only one woman was inside the building.

"*Aloha*," she greeted. "Welcome to Pu'ukohola. Feel free to look around and let me know if you have any questions."

"Thank you," Amalia replied. "Can I drive down to the temple?"

"Yes, but it is an easy walk from here. All downhill." She smiled. "Uphill to come back, of course, but you're young and healthy."

Amalia took an informational brochure. "I understand this temple was built by King Kamehameha."

"Yes. It was built and dedicated to Kukailimoku, the war god. This is the largest *heiau*, built by the king soon after he began his efforts to unify the islands through conquest."

"*Mahalo*." Amalia headed toward the door.

"By the way, when you get down to the beach, keep an eye out for the black-tipped sharks that swim here."

"I will."

Stopping at the car to grab her camera, Amalia then took the path that led to a steep but paved trail leading to the temple. The rocky terrain was planted with golden grasses and an occasional green bush or tree. At one point, Amalia paused beside a three-tiered wooden platform. On it rested what she had come to recognize as offerings to the ancient gods. She had seen them in several places, even on top of black lava boulders alongside the highway. Sometimes they were tiny towers of rocks, other times objects wrapped in ti leaves. Tempted to remove her lei and place it on the platform, she remembered it was *kapu*, or forbidden, for non-Hawaiians to either leave offerings or to disturb those left. It was considered a form of desecration.

Continuing down the trail, she encountered only one other couple on their way back up. The vista spread out before her, sloping gently down to the sea. The temple appeared, a long formation of black stones on top of a big hill. A sign forbade entrance to the *heiau*. She gazed up the path to structure, feeling dwarfed by its immense size, and she wasn't even standing near it.

She took several photos from different angles and continued on to the beach and the dark blue bay. The beach was an oasis of coconut palms and banyan trees. Under the trees the sand was soft and white, but nearer the water it became more rocky. The water lapped the shoreline and reflected the bright sunlight. Amalia squinted, looking for the black-tipped sharks. Every time she thought she saw one, it turned out to be a pointed rock. She picked up a fallen coconut and tossed it into the water, watching it bob in the gentle waves. She settled onto the warm sand, resting her chin on bent knees and wrapping her arms around her legs. The air was still and quiet. She felt at peace in this sacred place even though it had been built for a war god.

The minutes ticked by as she thought about her life these last two years — the loss of Kathy, the agonizing months in the rehabilitation hospital, the renovation of the old farmhouse. She'd grown and changed a lot in those two years. And now she had a chance to start a new life here, in this heavenly place. She felt a twinge of guilt as she thought of the friends and family she'd left behind. She'd sent them each a postcard when she first arrived, and nothing since. She wondered how Heather and Randy's commitment ceremony had gone and if Jacquie had found a new girlfriend yet.

Paige came to mind — her easy smile and hearty laugh, the dark blonde hair so similar to Kathy's, yet so different, and those mischievous brown eyes. Amalia shivered with pleasure as she remembered the feel of Paige's long, lean body and strong hands. She closed her eyes, imagining Paige's kiss, the softness of her lips, the thrust of her tongue.

She opened her eyes again. Paige had come to mean a lot to her in such a short time. If she wasn't careful, she would fall head over heels in love, if she hadn't already. She stood up and stretched. On impulse, she took the lei from around her neck and held it to her nose, breathing deeply of its sweet scent. With a kiss to one soft bloom, she tossed it into the water.

"Good-bye, Kathy," she whispered.

Chapter Twelve

By Monday morning, Paige couldn't stand it any longer. She'd spent the whole weekend in Mitch's house, waiting for Amalia to call. He'd tried to entice her out for more snorkeling or to the Kamehameha parade, but she claimed exhaustion and spent most of the time out on his balcony. She wrote more postcards home, reread the literature from the University of Hawaii, and even scribbled notes on a tentative Ph.D. dissertation topic. She also became good friends with Mitch's Abyssinian cats. Her only foray out was on

Saturday morning to run over to a clinic for an HIV test. Amalia hadn't called.

She didn't like feeling out of control. Women usually waited for *her* to call. She paced the living room and debated whether to call. Well, it wasn't so much that she couldn't call. It was just that she'd gotten the distinct impression on Friday night that Amalia wanted to be alone. She figured Amalia was feeling guilty about sleeping together so quickly.

"You can't make assumptions about other people's feelings," she berated herself. Then she laughed. Hell, she was always making those assumptions. And they were usually wrong.

"You're going to wear out my carpet," Mitch said, startling her. "Don't tell me you're stressed out."

"Don't sneak up on me like that!" At the expression on his face, she apologized. "Don't mind me, Mitch. I just fell hard for a woman and she didn't call me all weekend."

He sat on the couch and looked at her. "So that's why you've been moping around. Amalia."

"Yes. I think she gave me the brush-off Friday night after dinner. I'm not used to that happening to me."

He laughed. "I can tell the shoe is usually on the other foot. Guess you now know how all those women in your past felt."

"Well, yes."

"You just leave a trail of broken hearts behind you?"

She sat next to him on the couch. "I guess I have been pretty creepy. I just never met anyone who counted. And I think Amalia does. She's different from the others."

"Different? Are you sure you're not just sympathizing with her for what she's been through?"

She sighed and leaned back into the couch. One of the cats jumped up onto her lap, and she absently stroked him. "I don't know. I miss her. I can't remember ever missing a woman before."

He reached over, grabbed the cordless phone, and handed it to her. "Well, call."

"What if she doesn't want to see me again?"

"You'll never know unless you call. The most she can say is no."

She looked at him. "I don't take rejection well."

"You are one wimpy butch. C'mon, girl! Just call!"

Just then the phone rang, startling both of them. Paige cursed out loud as the cat raked his claws across her bare leg in his mad scramble for the floor. Mitch made kissing noises as he headed to the kitchen. She scowled at him.

"Hello?"

"Hi, Paige, it's me."

Her voice was enough to make Paige's heart beat faster. "Amalia," was all she could say.

"I'm sorry I didn't call this weekend. I was working through some things. I'd like to see you again."

"I was thinking that very same thing. Did you want to go somewhere today? Maybe Waipio Valley?"

"Actually, I heard about an artist's colony not far from here. Holualoa. I thought we might go there, maybe have lunch."

"I can pick you up within the hour."

"Good. See you then."

Paige wasted no time. She stuffed her Speedo and another change of clothing into her knapsack and raced out the door. She cooled her impatience and drove the speed limit. When she got to Hale 'O Kipa Pele, Amalia was waiting.

Wearing her blue-and-gold bathing suit under a pair of cutoffs, Amalia looked stunning. As usual, she'd left her hair down and loose despite the heat. The humidity made it curl gently against her shoulders. Her blue eyes lit up.

Paige got out of the car and gave her a kiss on the lips, then grabbed her and pulled her close, turning the friendly kiss into one of passion and want. Amalia reacted, pressing her body tightly to Paige, letting her fingers rake Paige's hair.

Paige groaned. "If you keep this up, we won't make it to Holualoa. Are your hosts home?" She nipped Amalia's sweet-smelling neck.

Amalia laughed and pushed her gently away. "Time enough for that later, sweetheart. And just who is it that started all this. Not I."

"I can't help myself. When I see you, I want to make love."

"Brent said we should check out the Holualoa Gallery on Mamalahoa Highway. Apparently, they've got fine art and great pottery."

Paige rolled her eyes. It wasn't pottery she wanted to get her hands on, but the sooner she took Amalia shopping, the sooner she'd be able to bring her home. Then she'd show Amalia her version of "fine art."

* * * * *

"So, what did you do this weekend?" Amalia asked as they drove up the road in her convertible. It was too nice a day for the Subaru. She let Paige drive, admiring her grip on the steering wheel.

"I did some preliminary work on my Ph.D."

"The whole weekend? You didn't snorkel or sight-see or anything? Not even the parade?"

"Didn't feel like it." She glanced at Amalia. "I did go to the clinic. Should have the results within the week."

Amalia patted Paige's thigh. "I'm not worried, but thank you."

"I hope you don't mind, but I made reservations for us tonight for the luau. If we get there early, we can watch them take the pig from the *imu*."

"*Imu*?"

"Yeah, the underground oven. It's supposed to be quite something to see. The cooks, or whatever they're called, use their bare hands to remove the hot rocks and then the pig."

Amalia leaned back in her seat, enjoying the feel of the sun against her face. "Did you ask Mitch about showing me a few houses?"

"Sure did. He said anytime you're ready. Do you have any ideas of where you want to live?"

"I spent yesterday in and around Hawi. It's really pretty up there, but I'm afraid it might be a bit too far from civilization for me. I don't want to live in Kailua-Kona, but maybe within thirty or forty minutes of it. Actually, Captain Cook wouldn't be too bad."

"Mitch says there are several houses for sale in his neighborhood."

Amalia had a sudden thought. "But you'll be going to school on Oahu."

Paige turned and grinned at her. "Don't worry, love, I'll just commute like Brent does."

Amalia felt a rush of pleasure. She hadn't really thought about it, but at that moment she realized that she did want Paige to live with her. Then she sobered. No, she might want that, but she would wait until she was absolutely sure. They'd only just met, and she wasn't about to commit. It had taken her too long to regain her independence. She studied Paige's strong profile. She appeared happy.

"Tell me, how did you get involved in marine biology? Iowa doesn't seem to lend itself to that. No oceans."

"I used to watch every Jacques Cousteau special that came on. It was so incredibly fascinating. Later, of course, came the Discovery Channel and TLC. Aunt Maggie eventually gave me a Greenpeace membership. That's when I really came to love whales."

Amalia had contributed to her local animal shelter, but she'd never gotten involved in international animal rights groups. Some of them seemed too extreme. "Aren't they a radical group?" she asked.

Paige glanced at her. "Greenpeace? I wouldn't call them radical. They do what's necessary to get their point across. Their members are very passionate. They put their own lives in danger to save the animals."

"My father always denigrated groups like that. He comes from a family of hunters, so I suppose he wouldn't understand."

"Do you hunt?"

Amalia smiled at her tone of voice. It was obvious

she found hunting repulsive. "My father took me once when I was about ten. It was enough to cure me of it." She laughed. "Actually, after that I made such a fuss whenever he went, he gave up hunting about five years later."

"I assume then that you can handle a gun?"

"Oh yes. I was a crack shot. My parents thought I could become an Olympian. Every parent thinks that, I suppose, when their kid excels at some sport."

They had entered the village of Holualoa. Paige finally found a parking space, and it wasn't a very long walk from one end of town to the other. Several art galleries and boutiques lined both sides of the street.

"Should we have lunch first?" Paige asked.

"Sure."

They found a little café. It was early yet for the lunch crowd, so they were seated immediately. They both ordered the ginger- and garlic-spiced Adobo chicken, a popular Filipino dish. It came with a crunchy green salad and rice. Amalia talked about the awards she'd won in pistol shooting, and Paige told her about the ones she'd won in swimming. Their growing-up years turned out to be quite similar.

After a dessert of coconut-pineapple ice cream, Amalia led the way out. She dragged Paige from one gallery to the next. The work was all excellent, and expensive. Amalia bought several carvings out of rare Koa wood to send back home. Paige ended up buying a painting on rice paper of a flying fish.

"I like the blues and greens," Amalia commented

when Paige showed her the painting. "It's interesting, too, how he caught the texture of the fish. Those wings look like butterfly wings."

The accompanying brochure explained how the artist had carefully covered the fish with paint, then pressed the rice paper against its body, leaving the multihued image.

Paige carefully rolled it back up and inserted it into a protective tube. "I haven't decided whether I'm going to keep it for myself or send it to Ma. She'll probably scold me for wasting my money."

They left the gallery and put all their packages in the car. Seeing a sign for a sale, Amalia led Paige up a steep gravel driveway to a private home. In the garage, shelves displayed handmade items — baskets, purses, pottery, and dried flower arrangements. One large basket was full of unshelled macadamia nuts.

A young woman came out of the house. "*Aloha*," she said. "Would you like to sample my macadamia nuts? We grow them ourselves right here."

Amalia and Paige both nodded. The woman opened a handful of nuts and presented them. The white, slightly greasy fruit was flavorful, much more so than what came in the familiar blue cans back home.

Echoing Amalia's thoughts, Paige remarked, "These taste so different from what I'm used to."

"Well, they are very fresh," the woman said, "and fresh always tastes better than canned." She smiled. "At least in my opinion."

Amalia slowly walked through the garage. The craft items were well made and unusual — not the same old stained glass, gaudy jewelry, crocheted afghans, and straw flower arrangements she saw on the mainland. She fingered a stalk of three wood roses.

"Roses for the lady?" Paige whispered in her ear.

Amalia turned and smiled at her. "I think these are so interesting. They grow like this, you know? They look like wood even on a live plant."

"But they don't smell as sweet as you," she replied.

Amalia smiled again and continued browsing, stopping now and then to pick something up for a closer look. She tried to show Paige another intricate basket.

Paige made a dismissive gesture with her hand. "You about ready to go?"

Amalia glanced at the young Hawaiian to see if she'd noticed Paige's impatient gesture. She was busy rearranging one of the shelves.

Before Amalia could say anything, Paige said to the woman, "I'll take that whole basket of wood roses."

"The basket too?"

"Of course."

After a quick exchange of money, Amalia and Paige headed for their car. Paige carried the basket of wood roses. She gave Amalia a suggestive grin.

"We've got a couple of hours before the luau. Shall we drop off these roses to your room?"

"I'm afraid," Amalia replied with a quick kiss, "that we'd never make it to the luau if we stopped there. Perhaps a stroll along Alii Drive instead?"

"You just want to do more shopping. Admit it."

Amalia laughed. "I did promise my friend Randy I'd send her some Hawaiian shirts. I found a store that will mail them to her directly."

In the car, Paige ran her hand along Amalia's bare

thigh. "I thought you might change into that lovely sarong you wore to dinner at the volcano." She leaned over and kissed Amalia long and hard.

"Mmmm," Amalia murmured, "you certainly know how to change a girl's mind. Let's go back to the B and B. Randy's shirts will just have to wait."

Chapter Thirteen

Amalia dressed with care. She and Paige had spent the rest of the afternoon in bed. Her body still tingled from their intense lovemaking. Paige was everything she had imagined and more. She shivered from the memory of Paige's mouth and hands and fingers. She had never felt quite so filled before.

She wore the rose-and-white sarong again, which contrasted nicely against her lightly tanned skin. She brushed her hair back on the left side and pinned in a spray of white gardenias. Their strong fragrance made perfume unnecessary. With one last glance in the mirror, she went to the living room to wait. She wondered if Paige would wear black leather again.

Brent gave a wolf whistle when he saw her. "You look fabulous," he said.

"Paige and I are going to the luau tonight. I wanted to dress the part."

"Once she sees you, she might not want to go."

Amalia felt the blush on her cheeks, but she didn't tell him that they'd already spent the afternoon making love. Paige had left before the two men had returned home. Suddenly nervous, Amalia poured a glass of iced tea to give herself something to do. She was surprised that Paige wasn't already there.

"How are you on reservations for the next few weeks? I think I'm going to begin my house search, but it could take a while."

Brent looked rueful. "Sorry, but we're full. We've got someone coming in on the fourteenth, next Monday, for your room. Two men arrive tomorrow for the Maile Room."

"Hmmm, do you think I should rent a house temporarily? Or would a hotel be better?"

Brent rested his chin on his hands. "I suppose it depends on how much money you're willing to spend. If money is no object, you'll probably find a house pretty quickly, which would make a hotel more practical. If you need time, I'd rent someplace."

Amalia sighed. "Guess I should have thought of all this sooner. I'll ask Mitch to start looking right away."

Just then, Paige knocked on the sliding glass door. She wasn't dressed in black leather this time, but in a bright flowered Hawaiian shirt and crisp blue jeans, obviously new. Her dark blonde hair was feathered back away from her face, which really showed off sun-lightened streaks of paler blonde. She opened the door and came into the living room. She eyed Amalia suggestively, her grin revealing her thoughts.

Amalia stepped over and kissed her. When their lips touched, fire ignited in her veins. She couldn't believe just how much this woman affected her. Could such intense emotion be sustained? Or would their relationship burn out before it even got started?

"We'd better go." She looked over and caught Brent smirking. "See you later, Brent," she said with a wave. He winked and she felt herself blushing again. She was sure her face matched the color of her sarong.

"I hope they have hula dancers," Paige said when they were on their way. She drove the convertible again.

"Of course they will. What's a luau without hula dancers? I'm planning on taking lessons myself."

Paige grinned again. "Now, *that* I'd like to see. You certainly have all the right moves."

"Oh, look!" Amalia suddenly exclaimed. She pointed excitedly. Silhouetted against the darkening sky amidst the scrub brush were the unmistakable shapes of donkeys — the Kona Nightingales. Amalia counted at least eight of them, two obviously young ones.

Paige turned off the highway in the direction of the Kona Village Resort. The road wound through the desertlike landscape, bringing them closer to the donkeys. She parked the car, and Amalia scrambled out with her camera. She wanted to walk toward them, but had to content herself with using her telephoto lens. Several of the animals looked right at her as she snapped a couple of shots. Satisfied, she got back into the car.

At the luau site, a hostess took their group on a quick tour of the grounds. As usual, the resort had its own irrigation system, and it almost felt like they were walking through a rain forest, but without the lush, earthy smell and dripping humidity of the one at Volcanoes National Park. There was no hotel here, only luxurious cottages of different architectural styles. The more expensive ones overlooked the ocean.

Paige leaned in close to Amalia. "Those cottages out at the edge go for two thousand a night," she whispered.

"Wouldn't it be grand to stay in one?" Amalia whispered back. She almost laughed at the incredulous look on Paige's face.

"Sure. If you're Ivana Trump."

Laughing, they continued with the group back to the entrance. They received their table assignments and head garlands of unnaturally pink plumeria blossoms. Paige frowned and took hers off as soon as they were out of eyesight of their jovial hostess.

"I thought you looked very sweet," Amalia said as she accepted the garland from Paige and wrapped it around her wrist. Because she had gardenias in her hair, she wrapped her own around one ankle.

"Sorry, but *sweet* is not in my vocabulary." She kissed Amalia's cheek. "At least when it comes to me. You, however, are the epitome of sweet."

They sat at their long table and ordered mai tais. A guitar- and ukulele-playing trio serenaded the crowd with traditional Hawaiian songs.

"They're going to uncover the pig now," one of the hostesses called out.

Amalia and Paige jumped up. A crowd had already gathered round the sand-covered *imu*. Four men, bare-chested and dressed only in cloth skirts, ceremoniously brushed the sand away and removed what appeared to be burlap bags. With their bare hands, they then removed steaming hot lava rocks and banana leaves. They put on quite a show, clapping their hands to dispel the heat of the rocks and whooping loudly. The crowd responded by clapping appreciatively.

The *imu* was not as deep as Amalia expected, and soon a ti-leaf-wrapped shape was exposed. As the leaves were removed, she saw not a whole pig with an apple in its mouth, but layers of juicy meat that had literally fallen off the bones. The men removed several more rocks before placing the meat on big wooden platters and carrying them to the buffet tables.

The crowd surged forward, heading back to the seating area. Once at their table, they had to wait their turn to be directed to the buffet tables, which were decorated with enormous arrangements of pink and red anthuriums and laden with serving trays labeled with names like *Tako Poki*, *LauLau*, and *Opihi*. The Asian influence was represented with familiar dishes such as sushi, teriyaki, and char sui. The aromas of all the dishes melded together in a pungent, delicious mix of roasted meat and spices and sea and fruit.

Amalia and Paige took their "plates," leaf-shaped bowls of monkeypot wood, and Amalia's mouth watered as she filled hers with mostly vegetable dishes, a slice of the *kalua* pig taken from the *imu*, plus bread and rice. Paige experimented a bit more, choosing to sample a little of everything. They returned to their seats. The group at the other end of the table was already in high spirits. Amalia counted several empty mai tai and piña colada glasses. She smiled across at Paige and then glanced around the big room.

"I don't see any other 'family' here, do you?"

"Not really. Hawaii is beautiful, but very hetero."

"Well, it is the honeymoon capital of the world. It's a shame that the antigay marriage ballot passed last year. Think of all the money that would have flowed into the state." She took a bite of sweet potato. "Still, I've always dreamed of living here."

Paige looked at her, puzzled. "Would you get married if it was legal for same-sex couples?"

Amalia leaned back in her chair. "Kathy and I talked about it a little. I don't know how I feel. Sometimes I think it's a good idea, and other times I think not. The benefits would sure be nice."

Paige shook her head. "I wouldn't."

"You seem very certain."

"Why imitate some heterosexual institution that by my reckoning rarely lasts? I know of gay couples who have been together longer than most straight marriages."

"Are your parents divorced?"

"No, but they're one of those rare exceptions."

Amalia only smiled. "Ready for dessert?" she asked.

They went to the dessert table, where Amalia chose *Haupia* pudding, a chilled coconut milk custard, and Paige decided on the banana and papaya *Po'e*. When they returned, the lights dimmed as the entertainment began. From the gentle sway of the Hawaiian hula to the dangerous fire play of the Samoan fire knife dance, Amalia found the performances both beautiful and electrifying. Paige's appreciative expression showed she felt the same, especially when the Tahitian dancers exhibited their athletic, sensual moves.

All too soon, the show was over. Amalia had taken several photos that she hoped would turn out. The lights had been dimmed the whole time, with the stage separated from the audience by a moat. They waited until most of the crowd had left before sauntering to the car. The warm air caressed Amalia's skin; a slight breeze ruffled her hair. She curled her fingers into Paige's palm, feeling completely comfortable and at ease.

Paige opened the car door. "Want to go for a walk along the beach?" she asked as she slid into the driver's seat.

"That would be nice." She looked into the sky. The moon was half full, covered with a gauzy wisp of cloud. The stars twinkled and shone. She wished she knew more about astronomy. She was sure there must be one or two zodiac constellations glimmering up above.

"Do you know about stars?" she asked, holding her hair so it wouldn't blow in her face.

"Starfish, yes. The ones in the sky, no. Why?"

"I wanted to find my sign."

"I can find the Big Dipper and Venus, but that's about it." She laughed. "You know, we never did ask each other the old 'What's your sign?' question."

Amalia laughed too. "Okay, I'm a Libra. How about you?"

"Scorpio."

"I should have guessed." She paused. "We're actually supposed to be quite compatible."

Paige turned briefly and smiled at her. "I have no argument there. Don't know if I've ever dated a Libra before."

"You've never bought a birthday present in October?"

"Nope. I only buy for my family, and they're all summer birthdays."

Amalia looked over at Paige, who stared straight ahead at the road. "You've never been serious enough about a woman to buy her a birthday present?"

"I know you must think I'm pretty awful. Yes, I admit my relationships have been casual at best. I was busy with studies. I moved around a lot."

"Are you afraid of commitment?"

Paige didn't answer, but deftly pulled into a parking space right along Alii Drive. She cut the engine and turned to face Amalia. "Look, you're gonna be disappointed if you want me to fit into some kind of lesbian mold. Call me a free spirit if you will, but that doesn't mean I'm emotionally damaged. It also doesn't mean I'll end up breaking your heart." She took a deep breath. "You've become very important to me in the short time we've known each other, but I think it's a bit early to be talking commitment."

Amalia felt a surge of anger. "I wasn't asking you for a commitment. That's the last thing I want from you, or anyone else." She turned away, looking out the window into the darkness, her arms folded across her chest.

The silence in the car lengthened. Amalia's breath felt tight in her lungs; her aortic aneurysm pulsed.

She unconsciously put her hands across her belly. When she felt the tears on her cheeks, she pushed open the door and got out of the car.

"What are you doing?" Paige asked, her voice low and urgent.

"I think I just want to be alone. Don't worry, I'll find a taxi to take me home."

Paige scrambled out of the car and came to stand beside her on the sidewalk. "I'm so sorry. I didn't mean to hurt you. Please, let me try to explain."

"There's nothing to explain. You and I shared something special for a few days, and now it's time to move on. That's what I came to Hawaii for, to move on."

Paige grabbed her arms. "Are you telling me you don't want to see me again?"

Amalia felt a sudden panic. No, she *did* want to see Paige again. The feeling was so strong, it almost frightened her. She shook her head and felt the tears flowing more freely. She hiccuped. Paige's fingers gently brushed the tears.

"Don't cry, sweetheart." She kissed Amalia's cheeks, then her mouth. The kiss was soft, tender.

Amalia felt the familiar stirring in her loins, as intense as that first time Paige touched her. It was hard to stay mad. She couldn't help but grab Paige's hair and increase the pressure of her lips. Paige moaned as she pulled her in close, pressing their bodies together. Oblivious to other tourists on the street, Amalia finally pulled away, breathing deeply.

"We should go home."

Paige smiled and took her hand. "I promised you a moonlit walk, and that's just what we're gonna do." She tugged Amalia toward the small beach.

Amalia's whole body protested. She wanted to feel Paige's mouth and hands as they drove her to ecstasy. How could Paige be so nonchalant now? But then Amalia saw the look in Paige's eyes. She was going to tease Amalia before she satisfied her. Amalia smiled. Two can play at this game, she thought as she slipped off her sandals. She pulled away from Paige and ran fully clothed into the warm ocean, where she dove under the water. Surfacing, she shook the wet hair out of her eyes. The sarong clung to the curves of her body.

Paige stood motionless on the sand, her restrained passion evident in her stance. Still in the water, Amalia ran her hands down her sides and licked her salty lips. Suddenly, Paige snatched off her shoes and ran splashing into the water. They came together under the light of the half-moon.

Chapter Fourteen

Amalia stretched languidly in the king-size bed. Light peeked around the edges of the window's heavy draperies, but otherwise the room was shrouded in darkness. Not feeling Paige beside her, she sat up quickly but lay back when she heard the shower. She sighed contentedly and snuggled into the blanket. Having left Hale Kipa 'O Pele two days ago, she was now staying in one of Kailua-Kona's generic but luxurious hotels. She'd spent most of last week house-hunting with Mitch and could tell that Paige was getting impatient.

"Good morning, sleepyhead," Paige said as she came out of the bathroom, vigorously toweling her hair. She sat on the edge of the bed and kissed Amalia's cheek. "I ordered room service."

"What are the plans for today?" Amalia asked, stretching again so the blanket fell away from her naked breasts.

"First, I give you multiple screaming orgasms . . ." Paige swiftly sucked in first one, then the other hardened nipple. Her hands drifted over Amalia's belly. "Then I give you some more."

Amalia moaned and arched her back, already willing and wet. Paige's mouth felt hot against her chilled skin. This woman was absolutely insatiable. Paige's mouth left a burning trail of kisses down her body, heading south. Amalia curled her toes as the sensations from Paige's mouth sent ripples up and down her spine. She had woken up turned on and ready, and urgently pushed Paige's head downward. Paige laughed quietly and complied. Her tongue and fingers performed their magic, sending Amalia over the edge. She screamed into her pillow. Embarrassed at the quickness of their lovemaking, she pulled Paige to her.

"I think you just broke your record," Paige laughed.

"Oh, God, I can't believe I just did that." Amalia felt her cheeks grow hot. She glanced at the clock. "What was it? All of ten minutes?"

"More like five."

"You must think I am so rude."

"Not at all, my sweet. So tell me, what were you dreaming about that you awoke so ready."

Amalia sat up. "I don't remember, but I wish I

did." She ran her fingers across Paige's sensitive collarbone. "How about I return the favor?"

"Room service will be here any minute, and I'm not quite as fast as you." She laughed again.

Amalia got out of bed and blew Paige a kiss. "I'm off to the shower then. Care to join me?"

Paige declined with a smile. When Amalia finished her shower, room service had arrived with their breakfast. Paige had ordered a fresh fruit platter, along with the traditional eggs and toast. They ate out on the balcony.

"I have an appointment with Mitch today at ten. He's got five more places for me to look at."

"Don't you think it's time for a break? We haven't done any sightseeing in over a week."

"We went on the whale watch."

Paige poured another cup of coffee. "That was all of four hours. I thought I'd take you back to the volcano. I think you're strong enough now to walk across the crater."

"I really need to get this house thing out of the way. Mitch knows now what I'm looking for, so it should go quickly."

Paige stood up. "I think I'll fly back to Oahu then. I have things I can do at the university, and I want to go to the aquarium in Waikiki. I'll call you, and when you're ready I'll come back."

Amalia held out her hand, but Paige ignored it. "We'll have plenty of time for sightseeing. After all, we'll be living here now."

"You mean, *you'll* be living here now. I'll be in some grad student housing in Honolulu."

Amalia looked at Paige, surprised she was so testy. "Listen, I know we haven't been spending as much time together, but it's only been a few days. And yes, I know you'll be in Honolulu most of the year, but that's just half an hour away."

Paige sat down and took her hand. "Sweetheart, you forget that I'm a student. I don't have much money left, and I'll have even less later. I'll need to get a student loan and some kind of part-time job."

Amalia thought about telling her exactly how much money she'd won in the insurance settlement but decided against it. Paige would never accept a handout. "You're right," she said instead. "Guess we'll cross that bridge when we come to it." She pushed away her plate. "Well, I'd better head over to Mitch's."

Paige caught the Aloha Airlines flight to Honolulu. She'd been tempted to take the one that left for the island of Molokai, but a quick review of her finances made her think better of it. Her grandmother's legacy would not last much longer if she continued spending indiscriminately. She was grateful to Mitch, who'd unobtrusively changed her status from paying client to welcome houseguest. She'd actually only planned to stay in Hawaii for two weeks, three at the most, and it was already week four. It was time to look for a job, but should she find one on Oahu or on the Big Island? Perhaps she was getting ahead of herself. Nothing was certain yet for school, and she didn't want to get locked into some lease that she couldn't keep. She decided to talk to Mitch when she returned about becoming a paying roommate. At least for the rest of the summer.

The plane landed with a bumpy thud, and Paige quickly caught a bus heading in the vicinity of the Coconut Plaza Hotel where she'd stayed before. She didn't bother to unpack, but soon found herself following the familiar path along the busy streets she'd taken when she'd first arrived in Hawaii. She even stopped at the same lei stand and bought an orchid lei that reminded her of the rain forest at Volcanoes National Park.

After a quick lunch, she walked to the Waikiki Aquarium, which she'd learned was part of the University of Hawaii. Diamond Head loomed before her. It seemed so out of place in the city. Where had Amalia gone to catch the tour to its summit? The zoo? Tree-lined Kalakaua Avenue was cool and wide open compared to downtown Waikiki. She found the aquarium easily, and it was much smaller than she'd anticipated. Home to some two thousand animals, including the endangered Hawaiian monk seal and the rare masked angelfish, it only took her about two hours to see the whole thing. It was certainly no Sea World, but Paige much preferred the small aquarium to the entertainment conglomerate.

Near the monk seal exhibit, Paige leaned over the low cement wall that separated the aquarium from the Pacific Ocean and found herself thinking of Amalia. What was she doing now? Had Paige made a mistake coming to Oahu? She fingered the delicate petals of her orchid lei. They were soft, like Amalia's skin. Their subtle flowery fragrance reminded her of Amalia's perfume. With a sigh, she turned her back on the ocean and felt her heart start beating faster. A slender woman with reddish blonde hair was heading toward the aquarium building. Paige took a step forward and opened her mouth to call out. Out of nowhere, two young children scampered over to the woman. They laughed and pointed excitedly at the ocean. When the woman turned, Paige saw that it was not Amalia. She felt suddenly lonely.

She returned to the main building and spoke with the director of the aquarium. He seemed interested when she told him she had a master's in marine biology and would be pursuing her Ph.D. at the university. Her hopes of employment were quickly dashed, however.

"Your credentials sound very impressive," he said, "but do you know how many people we get applying to work here? Actually, when you begin your studies at the university, it will be easier find work with one of our research or education programs."

"Well, I only asked on the spur of the moment." She shrugged. "I don't even have a copy of my résumé with me. Thanks for talking to me though."

"For right now, you might want to try at one of the many research vessels that anchor here. They're probably fully staffed for the summer, but they do have turnover, especially come fall."

"I guess it's everyone's dream to find work in Hawaii. I'm sure jobs are hard to come by."

He smiled encouragingly. "Well, if you're willing to settle for less until you find the job you want, opportunities do present themselves on occasion."

"Thanks again."

"Good luck."

She waved as she left his tiny office. She really hadn't expected a job to be waiting, ready to fall into her lap. She'd asked on a whim. She wondered what he meant by "settle for less." Was he referring to a retail or service-oriented job? Maybe she would check out the university's job postings.

She put school and work out of her mind as she strode up Kalakaua Avenue and back into the hustle and bustle of Waikiki. It was still too early, but tonight she would find that bar again — the one Judith and Jennifer liked. She was sure they had left the island long ago, but she could always hope.

Within three days of Paige's leaving the Big Island, Amalia found the perfect house. Near Captain Cook in the South Kona district, the island-style cedar home on ten acres boasted open, beam ceilings and stained-glass skylights. From the wraparound lanai, one had sweeping views of the Pacific Ocean and surrounding countryside, including the property's terraced mango and coffee groves. Behind the house was a lushly landscaped bell-shaped pool. Standing on the lanai, Amalia could smell the fragrant gardens.

With seven bedrooms and five baths, Amalia thought at first the house was too big, but as she walked through she knew she would buy it. It was freshly painted throughout in an alabaster white, and with the numerous windows was bright and airy. Hardwood floors gleamed, reflecting the colors from the stained-glass skylights. The gourmet kitchen was a chef's dream. Amalia decided when she saw it that she would have to hire a cook. Her meager cooking skills would be wasted here.

"We can probably go to settlement fairly quickly, especially because you're paying cash," Mitch told her as they drove away down the private driveway. "The owners had a buyer, but his mother got sick and he had to return to the mainland indefinitely. All the inspections and assessments have been done."

Amalia looked out the back window. The cedar house glowed warmly in the late afternoon sun. She wanted to move in tomorrow and said so.

Mitch laughed. "I guess you've had enough of hotel living. I'll contact the owners. I'm sure they won't mind if you move in before settlement."

"How long has it been up for sale?"

"About two years now. It's been empty more than a year, but they only renovated in the last four months."

She smirked. "Renovated? The new paint?"

He drove back out onto the highway and headed for Captain Cook. They were going to have dinner together at the Aloha Café. "It needed other work as well, but no one wanted to pay the three-hundred-thousand-dollar price tag and still have thousands of dollars worth of cosmetic repairs. They've done what was required, but didn't raise the price." He slowed to let a dog lope across the road. "We can negotiate them down, I'm sure."

"Where did they move to?"

"Back to the mainland. Malibu, I believe. I think they felt too isolated on the island, although the husband did have a private plane. They could leave anytime they wanted."

Amalia leaned back in her seat and stretched her spine. Out of habit, she placed her hand over her stomach. Her constant reminder of the accident pulsed softly. She noticed Mitch glancing at her hand.

"No, I'm not pregnant," she said, knowing she'd guessed right when she saw his face redden. "I had an

162

accident two years ago and I have a little souvenir of it."

"I . . . I'm so sorry. I can't believe I would think . . ."

She laughed gently. "And why not? Lots of lesbians are having kids these days. I won't be one of them though; you can count on that."

Clearly uncomfortable, Mitch changed the subject. "Are you going to tell Paige about the house?"

"I'm not sure she cares to know."

He glanced at her. "Did you two have a fight before she went to Oahu? Is that why she left?"

"Yes and no. She was irritated at how much time I was spending house-hunting. I also think she's feeling stressed about her money situation."

"Yeah, I got that idea too. I kind of took her out of the paying-client mode."

Mitch pulled into a parking space near the café. They sat out on the verandah and resumed their conversation after they'd ordered cold drinks — fresh carrot juice for her and mango juice for him. Amalia played with her spoon. "I want to tell her we don't have to worry about money, but I'm afraid she'll take it the wrong way. And besides, we haven't made any sort of commitment to each other. For all I know, I'm just a summer fling."

"Why would you think that?"

She shifted uncomfortably in her chair. "I know she's had lots of women. No mention of any long-term relationships. And she'll be going to school eventually, maybe even as soon as this fall."

"It sounds to me like you're trying to convince yourself without first talking to Paige. Do you care for her?"

The waitress arrived with their food. Amalia pondered Mitch's question as she poured ketchup over her French fries and onto her garden burger. "Yes, I do," she finally answered. "Surprisingly so." She read the question on his face. "I think I need to tell you the whole story."

She told him about her life with Kathy, the house they'd bought together in Maryland, and the accident that had claimed Kathy's life and made Amalia a wealthy woman. She'd not only received her own settlement, but also the one due Kathy's estate, all of which she invested wisely with the help of her father. She described the injuries she herself had suffered and the agonizing recovery afterward. He cried when she talked of Sheba's cancer and laughed at her stories about friends back home, especially Alexander. Through dinner and dessert and two lattés each, he let her talk. It was cathartic for her. When the saga ended, she felt cleansed and, for the first time, truly ready to put the past behind her.

Mitch reached for her hand and held it tight. "You are a remarkable person. And I think Paige knows that. You should call her."

Amalia smiled with genuine pleasure. "I think you're right, on all counts." She stood up. "C'mon, Mitch, I need to make a phone call."

Chapter Fifteen

The incessant ringing of the phone permeated Paige's consciousness. She reached across the warm body lying next to her in the bed and picked up the offending instrument.

"Hello, darling. Did I wake you?"

The sultry voice made Paige bolt up. She glanced at the clock — almost midnight. Her female companion stirred, sending Paige into a panic. If she woke up and said something . . .

She kept her voice low. "Amalia? This is a nice surprise."

"Listen, I'm so sorry we had that fight. I've missed you terribly. We need to talk. I can fly over to Oahu tomorrow if you'd like."

"I've missed you too." She cleared her throat nervously. "Actually, I was planning on returning in the next day or two. No need for you to come here."

"Your voice sounds a little strange. Are you okay?"

"Of course I'm okay — just a bit sleepy is all."

"Oh, I'm sorry I called so late. Just ring me as soon as you arrive in Kona. I'll pick you up at the airport."

"Thanks. Goodnight."

Paige hung up and leaned back into the pillows with a sigh of relief. If Ulrike had answered the phone . . . Paige didn't even want to think about what Amalia would have said. Probably good-bye for good. She felt suddenly guilty and tried to quash the feeling. "It's not like we have a commitment or anything," she said out loud.

"What's that, darling?" Ulrike murmured sleepily.

"Nothing," Paige answered as Ulrike snuggled against her.

The next morning, Paige was up and dressed before the other woman woke. She didn't want to take a chance on something happening between them again. She felt the guilty flush on her face. "A little late to think of that," she berated herself.

"Think of what?"

"Oh . . . just a project . . . um . . . that I needed to do," Paige answered and leaned over to kiss the comely Swede on the cheek. "How about breakfast?"

"Mmmm, I could have you for breakfast." Ulrike laced her arms around Paige's neck and pulled her down.

"Sorry, sweetie, but I have a lot to do today." She gently extricated herself from Ulrike's embrace. "And you have your cruise to catch up with."

"You're right," Ulrike acknowledged as she sat up and slid her amazingly long legs over the edge of the bed. The splendor of her naked body was enough to take your breath away, Paige thought. "You order breakfast while I shower."

Paige watched her as she headed for the bathroom. Her darkly bronzed body contrasted starkly with pale hair the color of expensive Champagne. Paige had met Ulrike in the same bar she'd met Jennifer and Judith. Sitting alone at a table with a martini, she'd stood out from the rest of the patrons. It turned out that she worked as a chef on a cruise ship and had had enough of heterosexual honeymooners. Sunday was her only night off, and when in port she liked coming to the bar for a dose of gay culture. Paige had immediately fallen for her Swedish accent and sleek, athletic body.

They'd not stayed long at the bar, but at least this time Paige had come prepared. Amalia wouldn't have to ask her to go to a clinic to be tested for HIV. Amalia. The thought of her made Paige flush guiltily once again.

When she heard the shower turn off, she quickly ran out of the room and downstairs. This hotel did not offer room service. She grabbed a couple of plates from the breakfast buffet, filling them with fresh fruit and pastries. She borrowed a tray and carried them upstairs, along with two mugs of steaming hot Kona coffee. Ulrike was dressed and waiting.

"Mmmm, smells good," she said as she took a mug and sniffed appreciatively. She took a sip. "I have enjoyed our time together, Paige. I will be back in three weeks."

Paige bit into a guava, trying to ignore the blatant invitation in Ulrike's incredible blue eyes. "I honestly don't know where I'll be in three weeks." She tried to laugh. "Back home in Iowa, for all I know."

"You feel bad about last night, I can tell. You have a girlfriend maybe?"

"I'm really sorry Ulrike. Well, not sorry . . . I mean . . . I don't know what I mean."

Ulrike leaned over and kissed her gently on the lips. She tasted sweet, a mingling of papaya and sugared coffee. Paige fought the urge to pull her back into bed.

"I must go now," Ulrike said with an understanding smile. "Thank you for a night worthy of paradise."

She left before Paige could stop her. Paige sat alone in her room and finished her coffee. She felt like a total jerk. She couldn't make up to Ulrike what she had done, but she could make it up to Amalia. The only question was, should she tell Amalia about Ulrike? Well, she had some time to think about it. Right now she had to go out and finish up her business with the university.

* * * * *

Thursday morning, Paige tried one last time to call Amalia from the airport. Still no answer at her hotel room. In the past two days, she'd been unable to reach Amalia or even Mitch. She'd tried Scot and Brent too, but they didn't know where Amalia was. She fought back an uncharacteristic panic as she dialed Mitch's number yet again. Her flight was leaving in half an hour, and she'd decided to alternate calling him and the hotel until the last possible minute.

"Hello?"

She felt a surge of relief when she heard his voice. "God, Mitch, where the hell have you been?"

"Nice to hear from you too, Paige. You don't sound like yourself."

"Do you know where Amalia is? I haven't been able to get ahold of her for two days." Over the loudspeaker, she heard her flight announced.

"I'm surprised she didn't call you."

"Call me? Call me about what? Is something wrong? Did she have an accident?"

"Well . . . God, I hate to tell you like this."

"Mitch!"

"She's in the hospital in Hilo. Some kind of surgery yesterday. It has to do with that aneurysm she has."

Paige sagged against the wall. She heard the last call for boarding but felt almost paralyzed. The blood seemed to roar in her ears. Mitch's worried voice penetrated through thick wool.

"Paige? Paige, listen to me. She's going to be okay."

"Can you pick me up at the airport?" she croaked. "I'm boarding now."

"Of course. And don't worry."

Paige managed to hang up the phone and make it through the gate just in time. The half-hour flight passed in a blur. Her imagination conjured up all sorts of nightmarish images worthy of a Clive Barker film — images of a bursting aneurysm that spewed precious blood from Amalia's body. Don't be absurd, she chided herself silently as she resisted the urge to chew her nails. Finally, the flight landed and she bounded off the plane and ran across the tarmac.

"Paige! Here!"

Mitch waved. She ran over to him. "How long will it take us to get to Hilo?" she asked, breathless.

"About four hours." He held her arm. "Don't you have luggage?"

"I'll get it later."

"You'll get it now," he said calmly yet firmly. "Amalia is not in any danger. This was not life-threatening."

Paige paced near the baggage claim. "If I'd known, I could have flown directly into Hilo. What happened? And why didn't she call me?"

Mitch laughed lightly. "I suppose it's because she didn't want to worry you. And from your reaction, I can't help but think she was right."

Paige stopped pacing and stared at him, a flash of anger making her body rigid. "She calls me and tells me she misses me, that I should let her know when I'm arriving so she can pick me up. And then I can't reach her for two days, almost three? She didn't think I would worry?"

"I'm sure she has a good explanation," he soothed.

"Calm down. Getting all worked up won't get us there any faster."

She felt the anger drain from her body. Mitch was right, and it wasn't doing any good to take it out on him. He was being a friend, driving her to Hilo when she was sure he had plans of his own.

"I'm sorry. Listen, I can drive myself to Hilo. You must have clients . . ." She shrugged.

"Nope," he said cheerfully, "I'm all yours for the rest of the day. Besides, I wouldn't trust you to drive."

She grabbed her bag and followed him to the car. During the drive, he refused to talk about Amalia's medical condition, instead telling Paige about the house Amalia had bought. He asked about her trip to Oahu and her prospects at the university. He clucked sympathetically at her job plight but could offer no immediate solutions. He even insisted on stopping for lunch, but Paige could only push her food around on her plate.

At last, they arrived at the hospital and Paige impatiently asked for Amalia's room. The nurse pointed down the hall. Mitch stayed in the waiting room. Paige paused before the door, looking in through the small window. The bed nearest the door was empty. In the other, Amalia seemed to be sleeping. An IV dripped into her arm, but no other medical equipment appeared to be hooked up. Paige gently pushed the door open and stepped inside. Amalia was not sleeping. She turned and smiled at Paige.

Paige hurried to the bed and knelt down, taking Amalia's cool hand into her own. She kissed it softly, catching a faint whiff of baby powder. "I've been so worried," she murmured. She stood and pulled a chair over. "Why didn't you call me?"

"I didn't want to worry you. I expected to be home by the time you got back."

"What happened? Why are you here?"

Amalia sighed. "I went in for a routine ultrasound on Monday and the doctor found that the aneurysm had grown significantly since the last time."

"Grown? How big? Is it dangerous?"

"Well, two to three centimeters is considered normal, but mine was approaching six. The doctor felt that the rate of growth had changed dramatically enough to require repair because I was at risk for a rupture." She patted Paige's hand. "I'm only in for about a week."

"A week? You knew I'd be home in a couple of days. How can you say you thought you'd be out before I got back?"

Amalia smiled wanly. "I wasn't sure. Your voice . . . the last time we spoke . . . You just seemed different."

Paige couldn't look Amalia in the eyes. She got up on the pretense of pouring her a glass of water. Amalia took it gratefully and sipped slowly through a bent straw.

"I think it was just the late hour," Paige finally said. "You woke me up." At least that part isn't a lie, she thought ruefully. "I'm sorry you had to go through this alone."

Amalia took her hand. "You're here now. That's all that matters. I do have one bit of bad news though." Paige glanced up sharply, but Amalia had a twinkle in her eye. "I'll have about six weeks of recovery time. No strenuous physical activity."

"You mean like hiking across volcanic craters?"

Amalia smiled. "Yeah, something like that."

Paige leaned down and kissed her. "I love you," she said.

"I'll bet you say that to all the girls," Amalia joked.

"No," Paige said seriously, "only to you." At that moment, she knew just how right that was. She'd never felt this way about anyone before, and even the thought of losing Amalia sent a panic through her. The mistrust she had, the fear, all seemed to vanish.

At that moment, a nurse came in. "She needs her rest now," he told Paige, looking pointedly at his watch. Afternoon visiting hours were over.

Amalia did look tired. Paige kissed her lightly on the lips, ignoring the nurse. "I'll be by later tonight."

"Evening visiting hours are from six to eight," he said.

After Paige left the room, Amalia sank back into her pillows with a tired sigh. She automatically put her hand across her belly. Instead of smooth skin, she felt a thick bandage. Her head ached, but she didn't want to ask the nurse for any Tylenol just yet. She cooperated patiently as he checked her vital signs and her IV. He seemed a bit concerned about her blood pressure, frowning as he made a note on her chart that hung at the foot of the bed.

"Would you like me to close the curtains?" he asked.

"Please."

He pulled the curtains, shutting out the late-afternoon sun. They rattled faintly on metal rings. Only the pale fluorescent light above the bed broke the darkness. The nurse shut the door quietly.

Amalia could already feel her headache diminish. She knew it was mostly from stress. Hospitals had a tendency to do that. She was proud of herself for making the quick decision to have the surgery. Her first reaction to the doctor's news had been to want to call her mother, and not just for comfort, but to make the decision for her. Instead, she had retreated to the hospital cafeteria, drunk two cups of bad coffee, and then gone directly to the doctor's office to sign the admission papers. She had called no one back home. Now she wondered if that had been a good idea. They'd be furious at her, and worried, as Paige had been.

Paige. Just the sight of her strong face had made Amalia's heart race. She'd missed her so much, but their last phone call had left her with a feeling of unease. She smiled. Paige had told her she loved her. Magic words. Her smile faded. It was too soon. How could love grow in such a short time? They'd known each other barely a month.

Technicolor images swirled in her head. Meeting Kathy at Randy and Heather's St. Patrick's Day party. Their first kiss. Finding their first tiny apartment together that summer. A senior year spent mostly in bed, and then college graduation. Cheering Kathy on at the Marine Corps marathon. Their first post-college jobs. Choosing Sheba at the animal shelter. Picking out wallpaper for the new house. Kathy laughing. The first time they made love. And the last. Then bright lights and darkness. And suddenly, Kathy's face blended into Paige's, with her bold smile and laughing brown eyes. Amalia could almost feel the touch of her hands. Her mouth. Yes, love could indeed grow.

Chapter Sixteen

Amalia looked around the living room bright with sunshine. Sheer white curtains on the windows blew gently in the breeze. With the help of a professional decorator, she'd kept the decor simple — white and gold with ruby red accents. The hardwood floor was buffed to a burnished glow, covered only in the middle of the room with an Oriental carpet of red and gold. Colorful and fragrant flowers — everything from luscious orange-gold hibiscus to the exotic and unusual red heliconia to virginal white orchids — spilled from vases and bowls stationed on every available horizontal surface. Black-and-white prints of Kim Taylor Reece's exotic hula dancers adorned the walls.

She could hardly believe she'd actually moved in at last. Her surgery had delayed things almost a month. The luxurious hotel room had become a prison in more ways than one. She smiled, remembering Paige playing nursemaid, trying so hard to hide her impatience. The doctor had forbidden any kind of physical activity, sex included, for at least three weeks. Paige had been solicitous and tender. Amalia chuckled. They'd tried to make love three nights ago, but Paige had been too nervous to continue. Amalia felt that her body had been primed ever since, and she had plans for tonight, their first night in the new house, even though it was not yet six weeks since her surgery.

She sat on the comfortable new sofa and riffled through the invitations she'd written earlier. She was having a housewarming party at the end of August, and she was giving the folks back home a month's notice. For some, she'd included first-class plane tickets. As a surprise, she'd even written one to Paige's friend Rory. She felt a touch of sadness, thinking of another young life cut short. She hoped the invitation would find Rory. Paige had given her his parent's address but told her about his nomadic tendencies.

"Amalia, you're not going to believe what I found!"

Amalia looked up, startled by Paige's sudden entrance and sending invitations scattering. Paige's face was flushed, whether from excitement or exertion Amalia couldn't tell. Her tall, lithe body was even more darkly tanned and muscular. She'd gotten a job on one of Captain Dan McSweeney's whale-watching boats, playing both guide and researcher. Her dark blonde hair was streaked with sun-kissed strands of pale gold. In its tousled state, she looked like she'd just gotten out of bed. It was a delicious thought.

She was distracted from her lustful musings when she noticed that Paige seemed to be cradling something in her arms. Whatever it was, it squirmed around like some sea creature with multiple arms. When Paige came closer, she saw it wasn't just one creature, but three tiny calico kittens, whose eyes were barely open.

"Where did you find those? And where's their mother?"

Paige's face fell. "She's dead. I heard the kittens, but it took me forever to find them, she'd hidden them so well." She pointed with her chin. "In that outcropping of rocks covered with the purple bougain-villea."

Amalia rose from the sofa and took one of the kittens from her. It mewed softly and stopped strug-gling, curling into the crook of her elbow and under her breast. "How do you know the mother's dead?" she asked, stroking the kitten gently with one finger.

"She was there with them. I think she'd been hit by a car." Paige shook her head. "She must have used her last ounce of strength to return to her litter."

"What are we going to do with them?"

"Keep them, of course." Paige headed for the kitchen. Amalia followed. "You've got plenty of room, and they'll keep the mongooses at bay." She poured milk into three saucers, and they placed one kitten at each. They drank ravenously.

"I've never had a cat. Only dogs. I don't know what to do with them."

Paige took her in her arms and kissed her. "I'll

teach you everything you need to know," she
murmured. Her warm mouth kissed Amalia in all the
sensitive spots on her neck and shoulders. She felt
goose bumps rise and couldn't help the low moan.
Paige chuckled. "Let's make our new housemates
comfortable and then you can show me your room."
She lifted Amalia's T-shirt and kissed her breasts one
by one.

Amalia's whole body reacted to Paige's mouth.
"Just leave them here with the milk," she said
urgently.

Paige chuckled again. The sound sent ripples up
Amalia's spine. "Give me five minutes, my impatient
one."

Amalia watched as Paige quickly tore strips of
newspaper and put them in a cardboard box whose
sides she cut low. She placed one kitten at a time in
the box, praising each one as it did its business. She
managed to find a basket from somewhere and lined it
with a couple of Amalia's new dishtowels. She placed
the basket in a corner of the kitchen and put the
kittens in it. They curled up together and seemed to
fall asleep immediately. Paige poured out more milk
and then turned to Amalia with a pleased smile.

"They should be okay now for an hour or two."

Amalia took Paige's hand and kissed her fingers.
"It might be longer than that." She led Paige out of
the kitchen and into the foyer.

"Wait!" Paige stopped Amalia from going up the
stairs. She swept Amalia up in her arms. "This is
something I've always wanted to do ever since I saw
Gone With the Wind," she said as she carried her up
the grand wooden staircase.

The bedroom was decorated in the blues, pinks,

and lavenders of an eastern sunset, something Amalia had chosen to remind her of home. The king-size bed was draped with white mosquito netting that Paige swept out of the way. Sweet plumeria blossoms scented the room.

Paige's touch was tender and gentle. She ran her fingers lightly down Amalia's scars, both old and new. She kissed them softly, as if in some way she could feel the pain that had caused them. Amalia trembled beneath her touch. It seemed that somehow Paige was different — almost as if she was making love to her for the first time. At last she gave in to the exquisite sensations.

It was the end of August. Amalia couldn't believe she'd been in Hawaii almost three months now. It seemed like only yesterday she'd arrived in Honolulu and then Kailua-Kona. So much had happened in that short time, not the least of which had been meeting Paige. The goddess Pele had certainly brought her good luck that night.

Amalia came in from the gardens just as the sun was setting. The living room was awash in a pale pink glow. With the lights turned down low and several pikake-scented candles burning, the scene was set for seduction. Over the stereo system, Hapa played and sang. Amalia had heard the duo of Barry Flanagan and Keli'i Kaneali'i interviewed on National Public Radio and couldn't get enough of their romantic Hawaiian music. Amalia moved through the room, arranging a flower here, moving a candle there. She was nervous. She wanted the party tonight to be perfect.

She smoothed down her blue and white sarong one more time and fingered her pikake lei. Pikake — the Hawaiian wedding flower. The wondrous scent of it both relaxed her and made her want hot, passionate sex. She could almost feel like a bride tonight. She smiled as she thought of the surprise she had waiting upstairs for Paige — a real Victoria's Secret fantasy.

A scampering of little feet made her turn. The three calico kittens — Radclyffe, Una, and Mabel — had grown quickly in four weeks. They swarmed and tumbled after each other, slipping and sliding on the slick hardwood floor. To Amalia, they all looked alike. She didn't know how Paige could tell them apart. They skittered around the corner like Roller Derby queens and disappeared.

She and Paige had had a nasty fight over the kittens when she'd found them clawing their way up her expensive white curtains imported from Scandinavia. Since then, Paige had been diligent about teaching them to stay away from the curtains, as well as off the furniture. Spray bottles full of water placed strategically around the house were used liberally by both women and by the household staff.

"Everything looks so-o-o marvelous!"

Amalia turned toward the arched doorway. Looking stunningly exotic in a brightly flowered sarong, her friend Heather stood framed in glowing candlelight. Barefoot, she wore deep pink bougainvillea leis around both ankles, one wrist, and her neck. In the week she and Randy had been in Hawaii, she'd already taken hula lessons, and tonight she was planning to surprise her lover with a performance.

Amalia walked over and gave her a big hug. "I am so glad you could come. It's been great having you here this week."

"It was so sweet of you to send plane tickets. And first-class too!" She spread her arms and sighed. "I could really get used to this."

"Randy's gone to the airport to pick up Rory?"

"Yes, and she took Alexander and Mitch along. What time is Paige getting home?"

Amalia looked at her watch. "Actually, I'm surprised she's not here yet. She supposedly asked to get off early today."

Heather strolled into the room, sliding her bare toes across the Oriental carpet. She sighed with obvious pleasure. "Maybe the whale watch was extra good today." She sat on the couch and fluffed the pillows behind her. "When Randy and I took it, all we saw were dolphins."

Amalia took one more turn around the room. She wanted everything to be perfect, and it was. The staff she'd hired had done an excellent job. She was a trifle worried about her first party. She was glad she'd decided to wait to invite her family over later — her mother had suggested Christmas — but this was the first time Paige met most of her friends. There'd been a little bit of reserve when Paige and Randy, also a butch, had met, but she'd gotten on great with Heather. After a week, however, she and Randy were already best pals. They'd gone snorkeling several times and on the manta ray dive.

She arranged a vase of hibiscus one more time and then joined Heather on the couch.

"I must say," Heather said, "you look awfully good. You're right, coming here was the best thing for you." She touched Amalia's arm. "Leaving all those memories behind."

"I didn't really leave them behind. They're with me now. Sometimes I still go places and think about how Kathy would have liked them, but the pain is gone. I don't cry at the mention of her name or the sight of her picture." She glanced at a framed photo that sat on one end table.

Heather smiled. "And I bet I know who helped. Paige is a very nice woman."

"I like her a lot."

"Only like?"

Amalia felt her face grow warm. "Okay, yes, Heather, I love her."

"Have you told her?"

"Well, no, not exactly."

Heather gave her a don't-you-think-it's-about-time look. "And does she love you?"

"She's told me that."

"You sound skeptical."

Amalia thought back a moment to Paige's disclosure of her liaison with Ulrike. It had hurt her at first, but she acknowledged that they'd not had a commitment and that things had been a little tense between them. She smiled, thinking of Paige's stammered confession and awkward but sincere apology. It had been hard to be angry with someone so obviously contrite.

"It's just that Paige has an interesting past. She's

never really had a commitment to any woman." And thinking of the anguish in Paige's voice when she had finally talked about Mrs. Anderson, Amalia thought she understood why.

Heather tossed back her long blonde hair. "Honey, she was just waiting for you. Personally, I'm glad you have Paige. Now I don't have to worry about Randy anymore."

Amalia looked at her aghast. Heather didn't really think she had anything to worry about, did she? "Oh, you," she said in mock ire when she saw Heather's smirk. "Randy's crazy about you."

"I know. But seriously, Paige is —"

"Paige is what?" said a voice from the doorway.

Both women looked over. Paige stood under the archway, the light from the foyer striking her dark blonde hair and bringing out its golden highlights. Her darkly tanned skin contrasted with her pure white T-shirt and shorts. Her brown eyes crinkled with laughter.

Amalia sprang from the couch. "Paige is wonderful and incredibly handsome," she said as she threw her arms around Paige's neck and brought her head down for a kiss.

"Mmmm, you kiss me like that again and you'll have to miss your own party." Her hands fumbled with the knotted tie of Amalia's sarong.

Amalia automatically pushed her body against Paige's. The touch of those strong hands was enough to make her weak. "I want you so much," she murmured for only Paige to hear.

Heather cleared her throat. "Um, girls, don't you think you should save that for later?"

They reluctantly pulled apart. Before they could

say anything, a male voice spoke. "Up to your old tricks, I see."

Paige whirled around, disbelief in her face. "Oh, my God, Rory!" Amalia could swear she saw tears in Paige's eyes as the two old friends hugged. "When did you get here?"

"This nice woman picked me up about two hours ago," he answered, waving at Randy. "It seemed to take forever for my luggage."

As Rory and Paige hugged, Amalia couldn't help but smile as she glimpsed Alexander hovering in the background, his arm draped casually over Mitch's shoulders. He'd arrived three weeks earlier, and he and Mitch had become quite the item. In fact, Alexander had moved from Amalia's house and into Mitch's. She figured he'd return to Maryland only long enough to settle his affairs and then be back in Hawaii. Paige caught her attention.

"Thank you so much," she said to Amalia, her voice husky with emotion. "You don't know how much this means to me."

"I think I do," Amalia replied. She could feel tears prickling her own eyes. She walked over to where Rory and Paige stood.

Paige kissed her. "I love you, Amalia Grant."

"I love you too, Paige Parker."

Beyond the window, the sun drifted easily into the dark blue Pacific.

LOOKING FOR NAIAD?

Buy our books at
www.naiadpress.com

or call our toll-free number
1-800-533-1973

or by fax (24 hours a day)
1-850-539-9731

A few of the publications of
THE NAIAD PRESS, INC.
P.O. Box 10543   Tallahassee, Florida 32302
Phone (850) 539-5965
Toll-Free Order Number: 1-800-533-1973
Web Site: WWW.NAIADPRESS.COM
Mail orders welcome. Please include 15% postage.
*Write or call for our free catalog which also features an
incredible selection of lesbian videos.*

STRANGERS IN THE NIGHT by Barbara Johnson. 208 pp. Her
body and soul react to a stranger's touch.   ISBN 1-56280-256-9 $11.95

THE VERY THOUGHT OF YOU edited by Barbara Grier and
Christine Cassidy. 288 pp. Erotic love stories by Naiad Press
authors.   ISBN 1-56280-250-X   14.95

TO HAVE AND TO HOLD by Petty J. Herring. 192 pp. Their
friendship grows to intense passion . . .   ISBN 1-56280-251-8   11.95

INTIMATE STRANGER by Laura DeHart Young. 192 pp.
Ignoring Tray's myserious past, could Cole be playing with fire?
ISBN 1-56280-249-6   11.95

SHATTERED ILLUSIONS by Kaye Davis. 256 pp. 4th
Maris Middleton mystery.   ISBN 1-56280-252-6   11.95

SETUP by Claire McNab. 224 pp. 11th Detective Inspector Carol
Ashton mystery.   ISBN 1-56280-255-0   11.95

THE DAWNING by Laura Adams. 224 pp. What if you had the
power to change the past?   ISBN 1-56280-246-1   11.95

NEVER ENDING by Marianne Martin. 224 pp. Temptation
appears in the form of an old friend and lover. ISBN 1-56280-247-X   11.95

ONE OF OUR OWN by Diane Salvatore. 240 pp. Carly Matson
has a secret. So does Lela Johns.   ISBN 1-56280-243-7   11.95

DOUBLE TAKEOUT by Tracey Richardson. 176 pp. 3rd Stevie
Houston mystery.   ISBN 1-56280-244-5   11.95

CAPTIVE HEART by Frankie J. Jones. 176 pp. Love in the
fast lane or heartside romance?   ISBN 1-56280-258-5   11.95

WICKED GOOD TIME by Diana Tremain Braund. 224 pp. In
charge at work, out of control in her heart.   ISBN 1-56280-241-0   11.95

SNAKE EYES by Pat Welch. 256 pp. 7th Helen Black mystery.
ISBN 1-56280-242-9   11.95

CHANGE OF HEART by Linda Hill. 176 pp. High fashion and love in a glamorous world. ISBN 1-56280-238-0   11.95

UNSTRUNG HEART by Robbi Sommers. 176 pp. Putting life in order again. ISBN 1-56280-239-9   11.95

BIRDS OF A FEATHER by Jackie Calhoun. 240 pp. Life begins with love. ISBN 1-56280-240-2   11.95

THE DRIVE by Trisha Todd. 176 pp. The star of *Claire of the Moon* tells all! ISBN 1-56280-237-2   11.95

BOTH SIDES by Saxon Bennett. 240 pp. A community of women falling in and out of love. ISBN 1-56280-236-4   11.95

WATERMARK by Karin Kallmaker. 256 pp. One burning question . . . how to lead her back to love? ISBN 1-56280-235-6   11.95

THE OTHER WOMAN by Ann O'Leary. 240 pp. Her roguish way draws women like a magnet. ISBN 1-56280-234-8   11.95

SILVER THREADS by Lyn Denison. 208 pp. Finding her way back to love . . . ISBN 1-56280-231-3   11.95

CHIMNEY ROCK BLUES by Janet McClellan. 224 pp. 4th Tru North mystery. ISBN 1-56280-233-X   11.95

OMAHA'S BELL by Penny Hayes. 208 pp. Orphaned Keeley Delaney woos the lovely Prudence Morris. ISBN 1-56280-232-1   11.95

SIXTH SENSE by Kate Calloway. 224 pp. 6th Cassidy James mystery. ISBN 1-56280-228-3   11.95

DAWN OF THE DANCE by Marianne K. Martin. 224 pp. A dance with an old friend, nothing more . . . yeah! ISBN 1-56280-229-1   11.95

WEDDING BELL BLUES by Julia Watts. 240 pp. Love, family, and a recipe for success. ISBN 1-56280-230-5   11.95

THOSE WHO WAIT by Peggy J. Herring. 160 pp. Two sisters . . . in love with the same woman. ISBN 1-56280-223-2   11.95

WHISPERS IN THE WIND by Frankie J. Jones. 192 pp. "If you don't want this," she whispered, "all you have to say is 'stop.' " ISBN 1-56280-226-7   11.95

WHEN SOME BODY DISAPPEARS by Therese Szymanski. 192 pp. 3rd Brett Higgins mystery. ISBN 1-56280-227-5   11.95

THE WAY LIFE SHOULD BE by Diana Braund. 240 pp. Which one will teach her the true meaning of love? ISBN 1-56280-221-6   11.95

UNTIL THE END by Kaye Davis. 256pp. 3rd Maris Middleton mystery. ISBN 1-56280-222-4   11.95

FIFTH WHEEL by Kate Calloway. 224 pp. 5th Cassidy James mystery. ISBN 1-56280-218-6   11.95

JUST YESTERDAY by Linda Hill. 176 pp. Reliving all the passion of yesterday. ISBN 1-56280-219-4   11.95

THE TOUCH OF YOUR HAND edited by Barbara Grier and
Christine Cassidy. 304 pp. Erotic love stories by Naiad Press
authors.   ISBN 1-56280-220-8   14.95

WINDROW GARDEN by Janet McClellan. 192 pp. They discover
a passion they never dreamed possible.   ISBN 1-56280-216-X   11.95

PAST DUE by Claire McNab. 224 pp. 10th Carol Ashton
mystery.   ISBN 1-56280-217-8   11.95

CHRISTABEL by Laura Adams. 224 pp. Two captive hearts and
the passion that will set them free.   ISBN 1-56280-214-3   11.95

PRIVATE PASSIONS by Laura DeHart Young. 192 pp. An
unforgettable new portrait of lesbian love . . .   ISBN 1-56280-215-1   11.95

BAD MOON RISING by Barbara Johnson. 208 pp. 2nd Colleen
Fitzgerald mystery.   ISBN 1-56280-211-9   11.95

RIVER QUAY by Janet McClellan. 208 pp. 3rd Tru North
mystery.   ISBN 1-56280-212-7   11.95

ENDLESS LOVE by Lisa Shapiro. 272 pp. To believe, once
again, that love can be forever.   ISBN 1-56280-213-5   11.95

FALLEN FROM GRACE by Pat Welch. 256 pp. 6th Helen Black
mystery.   ISBN 1-56280-209-7   11.95

THE NAKED EYE by Catherine Ennis. 208 pp. Her lover in the
camera's eye . . .   ISBN 1-56280-210-0   11.95

OVER THE LINE by Tracey Richardson. 176 pp. 2nd Stevie
Houston mystery.   ISBN 1-56280-202-X   11.95

JULIA'S SONG by Ann O'Leary. 208 pp. Strangely
disturbing . . . strangely exciting.   ISBN 1-56280-197-X   11.95

LOVE IN THE BALANCE by Marianne K. Martin. 256 pp.
Weighing the costs of love . . .   ISBN 1-56280-199-6   11.95

PIECE OF MY HEART by Julia Watts. 208 pp. All the
stuff that dreams are made of —   ISBN 1-56280-206-2   11.95

MAKING UP FOR LOST TIME by Karin Kallmaker. 240 pp.
Nobody does it better . . .   ISBN 1-56280-196-1   11.95

GOLD FEVER by Lyn Denison. 224 pp. By author of *Dream
Lover.*   ISBN 1-56280-201-1   11.95

WHEN THE DEAD SPEAK by Therese Szymanski. 224 pp. 2nd
Brett Higgins mystery.   ISBN 1-56280-198-8   11.95

FOURTH DOWN by Kate Calloway. 240 pp. 4th Cassidy James
mystery.   ISBN 1-56280-205-4   11.95

A MOMENT'S INDISCRETION by Peggy J. Herring. 176 pp.
There's a fine line between love and lust . . .   ISBN 1-56280-194-5   11.95

CITY LIGHTS/COUNTRY CANDLES by Penny Hayes. 208 pp.
About the women she has known . . .   ISBN 1-56280-195-3   11.95

POSSESSIONS by Kaye Davis. 240 pp. 2nd Maris Middleton
mystery.   ISBN 1-56280-192-9   11.95

A QUESTION OF LOVE by Saxon Bennett. 208 pp. Every
woman is granted one great love.   ISBN 1-56280-205-4   11.95

RHYTHM TIDE by Frankie J. Jones. 160 pp. . . . to desire
passionately and be passionately desired.   ISBN 1-56280-189-9   11.95

PENN VALLEY PHOENIX by Janet McClellan. 208 pp. 2nd
Tru North Mystery.   ISBN 1-56280-200-3   11.95

BY RESERVATION ONLY by Jackie Calhoun. 240 pp. A
chance for true happiness.   ISBN 1-56280-191-0   11.95

OLD BLACK MAGIC by Jaye Maiman. 272 pp. 9th Robin
Miller mystery.   ISBN 1-56280-175-9   11.95

LEGACY OF LOVE by Marianne K. Martin. 240 pp. Women
will do anything for her . . .   ISBN 1-56280-184-8   11.95

LETTING GO by Ann O'Leary. 160 pp. Laura, at 39, in love
with 23-year-old Kate.   ISBN 1-56280-183-X   11.95

LADY BE GOOD edited by Barbara Grier and Christine Cassidy.
288 pp. Erotic stories by Naiad Press authors. ISBN 1-56280-180-5   14.95

CHAIN LETTER by Claire McNab. 288 pp. 9th Carol Ashton
mystery.   ISBN 1-56280-181-3   11.95

NIGHT VISION by Laura Adams. 256 pp. Erotic fantasy romance
by "famous" author.   ISBN 1-56280-182-1   11.95

SEA TO SHINING SEA by Lisa Shapiro. 256 pp. Unable to resist
the raging passion . . .   ISBN 1-56280-177-5   11.95

THIRD DEGREE by Kate Calloway. 224 pp. 3rd Cassidy James
mystery.   ISBN 1-56280-185-6   11.95

WHEN THE DANCING STOPS by Therese Szymanski. 272 pp.
1st Brett Higgins mystery.   ISBN 1-56280-186-4   11.95

PHASES OF THE MOON by Julia Watts. 192 pp. . . . . hungry
for everything life has to offer.   ISBN 1-56280-176-7   11.95

BABY IT'S COLD by Jaye Maiman. 256 pp. 5th Robin Miller
mystery.   ISBN 1-56280-156-2   10.95

CLASS REUNION by Linda Hill. 176 pp. The girl from her
past . . .   ISBN 1-56280-178-3   11.95

DREAM LOVER by Lyn Denison. 224 pp. A soft, sensuous,
romantic fantasy.   ISBN 1-56280-173-1   11.95

FORTY LOVE by Diana Simmonds. 288 pp. Joyous, heart-
warming romance.   ISBN 1-56280-171-6   11.95

IN THE MOOD by Robbi Sommers. 160 pp. The queen of
erotic tension!   ISBN 1-56280-172-4   11.95

SWIMMING CAT COVE by Lauren Douglas. 192 pp. 2nd
Allison O'Neil Mystery.   ISBN 1-56280-168-6   11.95

THE LOVING LESBIAN by Claire McNab and Sharon Gedan. 240 pp. Explore the experiences that make lesbian love unique.

ISBN 1-56280-169-4   14.95

COURTED by Celia Cohen. 160 pp. Sparkling romantic encounter.   ISBN 1-56280-166-X   11.95

SEASONS OF THE HEART by Jackie Calhoun. 240 pp. Romance through the years.   ISBN 1-56280-167-8   11.95

K. C. BOMBER by Janet McClellan. 208 pp. 1st Tru North mystery.   ISBN 1-56280-157-0   11.95

LAST RITES by Tracey Richardson. 192 pp. 1st Stevie Houston mystery.   ISBN 1-56280-164-3   11.95

EMBRACE IN MOTION by Karin Kallmaker. 256 pp. A whirlwind love affair.   ISBN 1-56280-165-1   11.95

HOT CHECK by Peggy J. Herring. 192 pp. Will workaholic Alice fall for guitarist Ricky?   ISBN 1-56280-163-5   11.95

OLD TIES by Saxon Bennett. 176 pp. Can Cleo surrender to a passionate new love?   ISBN 1-56280-159-7   11.95

LOVE ON THE LINE by Laura DeHart Young. 176 pp. Will Stef win Kay's heart?   ISBN 1-56280-162-7   11.95

DEVIL'S LEG CROSSING by Kaye Davis. 192 pp. 1st Maris Middleton mystery.   ISBN 1-56280-158-9   11.95

COSTA BRAVA by Marta Balletbo Coll. 144 pp. Read the book, see the movie!   ISBN 1-56280-153-8   11.95

MEETING MAGDALENE & OTHER STORIES by Marilyn Freeman. 144 pp. Read the book, see the movie!

ISBN 1-56280-170-8   11.95

SECOND FIDDLE by Kate 208 pp. 2nd P.I. Cassidy James mystery.   ISBN 1-56280-169-6   11.95

LAUREL by Isabel Miller. 128 pp. By the author of the beloved *Patience and Sarah*.   ISBN 1-56280-146-5   10.95

LOVE OR MONEY by Jackie Calhoun. 240 pp. The romance of real life.   ISBN 1-56280-147-3   10.95

SMOKE AND MIRRORS by Pat Welch. 224 pp. 5th Helen Black Mystery.   ISBN 1-56280-143-0   10.95

DANCING IN THE DARK edited by Barbara Grier & Christine Cassidy. 272 pp. Erotic love stories by Naiad Press authors.

ISBN 1-56280-144-9   14.95

TIME AND TIME AGAIN by Catherine Ennis. 176 pp. Passionate love affair.   ISBN 1-56280-145-7   10.95

PAXTON COURT by Diane Salvatore. 256 pp. Erotic and wickedly funny contemporary tale about the business of learning to live together.   ISBN 1-56280-114-7   10.95

MISS PETTIBONE AND MISS McGRAW by Brenda Weathers.
208 pp. A charming ghostly love story.   ISBN 1-56280-151-1   10.95

CHANGES by Jackie Calhoun. 208 pp. Involved romance and
relationships.   ISBN 1-56280-083-3   10.95

FAIR PLAY by Rose Beecham. 256 pp. An Amanda Valentine
Mystery.   ISBN 1-56280-081-7   10.95

PAYBACK by Celia Cohen. 176 pp. A gripping thriller of romance,
revenge and betrayal.   ISBN 1-56280-084-1   10.95

THE BEACH AFFAIR by Barbara Johnson. 224 pp. Sizzling
summer romance/mystery/intrigue.   ISBN 1-56280-090-6   10.95

GETTING THERE by Robbi Sommers. 192 pp. Nobody does it
like Robbi!   ISBN 1-56280-099-X   10.95

FINAL CUT by Lisa Haddock. 208 pp. 2nd Carmen Ramirez
Mystery.   ISBN 1-56280-088-4   10.95

FLASHPOINT by Katherine V. Forrest. 256 pp. A Lesbian
blockbuster!   ISBN 1-56280-079-5   10.95

CLAIRE OF THE MOON by Nicole Conn. Audio Book —
Read by Marianne Hyatt.   ISBN 1-56280-113-9   13.95

FOR LOVE AND FOR LIFE: INTIMATE PORTRAITS OF
LESBIAN COUPLES by Susan Johnson. 224 pp.
     ISBN 1-56280-091-4   14.95

DEVOTION by Mindy Kaplan. 192 pp. See the movie — read
the book!   ISBN 1-56280-093-0   10.95

SOMEONE TO WATCH by Jaye Maiman. 272 pp. 4th Robin
Miller Mystery.   ISBN 1-56280-095-7   10.95

GREENER THAN GRASS by Jennifer Fulton. 208 pp. A young
woman — a stranger in her bed.   ISBN 1-56280-092-2   10.95

TRAVELS WITH DIANA HUNTER by Regine Sands. Erotic
lesbian romp. Audio Book (2 cassettes)   ISBN 1-56280-107-4   13.95

CABIN FEVER by Carol Schmidt. 256 pp. Sizzling suspense
and passion.   ISBN 1-56280-089-1   10.95

THERE WILL BE NO GOODBYES by Laura DeHart Young. 192
pp. Romantic love, strength, and friendship.   ISBN 1-56280-103-1   10.95

FAULTLINE by Sheila Ortiz Taylor. 144 pp. Joyous comic
lesbian novel.   ISBN 1-56280-108-2   9.95

OPEN HOUSE by Pat Welch. 176 pp. 4th Helen Black Mystery.
     ISBN 1-56280-102-3   10.95

ONCE MORE WITH FEELING by Peggy J. Herring. 240 pp.
Lighthearted, loving romantic adventure.   ISBN 1-56280-089-2   11.95

WHISPERS by Kris Bruyer. 176 pp. Romantic ghost story.
     ISBN 1-56280-082-5   10.95

PAINTED MOON by Karin Kallmaker. 224 pp. Delicious
Kallmaker romance. ISBN 1-56280-075-2 11.95

THE MYSTERIOUS NAIAD edited by Katherine V. Forrest &
Barbara Grier. 320 pp. Love stories by Naiad Press authors.
ISBN 1-56280-074-4 14.95

DAUGHTERS OF A CORAL DAWN by Katherine V. Forrest.
240 pp. Tenth Anniversay Edition. ISBN 1-56280-104-X 11.95

BODY GUARD by Claire McNab. 208 pp. 6th Carol Ashton
Mystery. ISBN 1-56280-073-6 11.95

CACTUS LOVE by Lee Lynch. 192 pp. Stories by the beloved
storyteller. ISBN 1-56280-071-X 9.95

SECOND GUESS by Rose Beecham. 216 pp. An Amanda
Valentine Mystery. ISBN 1-56280-069-8 9.95

A RAGE OF MAIDENS by Lauren Wright Douglas. 240 pp.
6th Caitlin Reece Mystery. ISBN 1-56280-068-X 10.95

TRIPLE EXPOSURE by Jackie Calhoun. 224 pp. Romantic
drama involving many characters. ISBN 1-56280-067-1 10.95

PERSONAL ADS by Robbi Sommers. 176 pp. Sizzling short
stories. ISBN 1-56280-059-0 11.95

CROSSWORDS by Penny Sumner. 256 pp. 2nd Victoria Cross
Mystery. ISBN 1-56280-064-7 9.95

SWEET CHERRY WINE by Carol Schmidt. 224 pp. A novel of
suspense. ISBN 1-56280-063-9 9.95

CERTAIN SMILES by Dorothy Tell. 160 pp. Erotic short stories.
ISBN 1-56280-066-3 9.95

EDITED OUT by Lisa Haddock. 224 pp. 1st Carmen Ramirez
Mystery. ISBN 1-56280-077-9 9.95

SMOKEY O by Celia Cohen. 176 pp. Relationships on the
playing field. ISBN 1-56280-057-4 9.95

KATHLEEN O'DONALD by Penny Hayes. 256 pp. Rose and
Kathleen find each other and employment in 1909 NYC.
ISBN 1-56280-070-1 9.95

STAYING HOME by Elisabeth Nonas. 256 pp. Molly and Alix
want a baby . . . or do they? ISBN 1-56280-076-0 10.95

TRUE LOVE by Jennifer Fulton. 240 pp. Six lesbians searching
for love in all the "right" places. ISBN 1-56280-035-3 11.95

KEEPING SECRETS by Penny Mickelbury. 208 pp. 1st Gianna
Maglione Mystery. ISBN 1-56280-052-3 9.95

THE ROMANTIC NAIAD edited by Katherine V. Forrest &
Barbara Grier. 336 pp. Love stories by Naiad Press authors.
ISBN 1-56280-054-X 14.95

UNDER MY SKIN by Jaye Maiman. 336 pp. 3rd Robin Miller
Mystery.   ISBN 1-56280-049-3.   11.95

CAR POOL by Karin Kallmaker. 272pp. Lesbians on wheels
and then some!   ISBN 1-56280-048-5   11.95

NOT TELLING MOTHER: STORIES FROM A LIFE by Diane
Salvatore. 176 pp. Her 3rd novel.   ISBN 1-56280-044-2   9.95

GOBLIN MARKET by Lauren Wright Douglas. 240pp. 5th Caitlin
Reece Mystery.   ISBN 1-56280-047-7   10.95

FRIENDS AND LOVERS by Jackie Calhoun. 224 pp. Midwestern Lesbian lives and loves.   ISBN 1-56280-041-8   11.95

BEHIND CLOSED DOORS by Robbi Sommers. 192 pp. Hot,
erotic short stories.   ISBN 1-56280-039-6   11.95

CLAIRE OF THE MOON by Nicole Conn. 192 pp. See the
movie — read the book!   ISBN 1-56280-038-8   11.95

SILENT HEART by Claire McNab. 192 pp. Exotic Lesbian
romance.   ISBN 1-56280-036-1   11.95

SAVING GRACE by Jennifer Fulton. 240 pp. Adventure and
romantic entanglement.   ISBN 1-56280-051-5   11.95

CURIOUS WINE by Katherine V. Forrest. 176 pp. Tenth Anniver-
sary Edition. The most popular contemporary Lesbian love story.
                                      ISBN 1-56280-053-1   11.95
          Audio Book (2 cassettes)   ISBN 1-56280-105-8   13.95

CHAUTAUQUA by Catherine Ennis. 192 pp. Exciting, romantic
adventure.   ISBN 1-56280-032-9   9.95

A PROPER BURIAL by Pat Welch. 192 pp. 3rd Helen Black
Mystery.   ISBN 1-56280-033-7   9.95

SILVERLAKE HEAT: A Novel of Suspense by Carol Schmidt.
240 pp. Rhonda is as hot as Laney's dreams. ISBN 1-56280-031-0   9.95

LOVE, ZENA BETH by Diane Salvatore. 224 pp. The most talked
about lesbian novel of the nineties! ISBN 1-56280-030-2   10.95

A DOORYARD FULL OF FLOWERS by Isabel Miller. 160 pp.
Stories incl. 2 sequels to *Patience and Sarah*. ISBN 1-56280-029-9   9.95

MURDER BY TRADITION by Katherine V. Forrest. 288 pp. 4th
Kate Delafield Mystery.   ISBN 1-56280-002-7   11.95

THE EROTIC NAIAD edited by Katherine V. Forrest & Barbara
Grier. 224 pp. Love stories by Naiad Press authors.
                                      ISBN 1-56280-026-4   14.95

DEAD CERTAIN by Claire McNab. 224 pp. 5th Carol Ashton
Mystery.   ISBN 1-56280-027-2   9.95

CRAZY FOR LOVING by Jaye Maiman. 320 pp. 2nd Robin Miller
Mystery.   ISBN 1-56280-025-6   11.95

UNCERTAIN COMPANIONS by Robbi Sommers. 204 pp.
Steamy, erotic novel.   ISBN 1-56280-017-5   11.95

A TIGER'S HEART by Lauren W. Douglas. 240 pp. 4th Caitlin
Reece Mystery.   ISBN 1-56280-018-3   9.95

PAPERBACK ROMANCE by Karin Kallmaker. 256 pp. A
delicious romance.   ISBN 1-56280-019-1   10.95

THE LAVENDER HOUSE MURDER by Nikki Baker. 224 pp.
2nd Virginia Kelly Mystery.   ISBN 1-56280-012-4   9.95

PASSION BAY by Jennifer Fulton. 224 pp. Passionate romance,
virgin beaches, tropical skies.   ISBN 1-56280-028-0   10.95

STICKS AND STONES by Jackie Calhoun. 208 pp. Contemporary
lesbian lives and loves.   ISBN 1-56280-020-5   9.95
Audio Book (2 cassettes)   ISBN 1-56280-106-6   13.95

UNDER THE SOUTHERN CROSS by Claire McNab. 192 pp.
Romantic nights Down Under.   ISBN 1-56280-011-6   11.95

GRASSY FLATS by Penny Hayes. 256 pp. Lesbian romance in
the '30s.   ISBN 1-56280-010-8   9.95

THE END OF APRIL by Penny Sumner. 240 pp. 1st Victoria
Cross Mystery.   ISBN 1-56280-007-8   8.95

KISS AND TELL by Robbi Sommers. 192 pp. Scorching stories
by the author of *Pleasures*.   ISBN 1-56280-005-1   11.95

STILL WATERS by Pat Welch. 208 pp. 2nd Helen Black Mystery.
                                               ISBN 0-941483-97-5   9.95

TO LOVE AGAIN by Evelyn Kennedy. 208 pp. Wildly romantic
love story.   ISBN 0-941483-85-1   11.95

IN THE GAME by Nikki Baker. 192 pp. 1st Virginia Kelly
Mystery.   ISBN 1-56280-004-3   9.95

STRANDED by Camarin Grae. 320 pp. Entertaining, riveting
adventure.   ISBN 0-941483-99-1   9.95

THE DAUGHTERS OF ARTEMIS by Lauren Wright Douglas.
240 pp. 3rd Caitlin Reece Mystery.   ISBN 0-941483-95-9   9.95

CLEARWATER by Catherine Ennis. 176 pp. Romantic secrets
of a small Louisiana town.   ISBN 0-941483-65-7   8.95

THE HALLELUJAH MURDERS by Dorothy Tell. 176 pp. 2nd
Poppy Dillworth Mystery.   ISBN 0-941483-88-6   8.95

BENEDICTION by Diane Salvatore. 272 pp. Striking, contem-
porary romantic novel.   ISBN 0-941483-90-8   11.95

COP OUT by Claire McNab. 208 pp. 4th Carol Ashton Mystery.
                                               ISBN 0-941483-84-3   10.95

THE BEVERLY MALIBU by Katherine V. Forrest. 288 pp. 3rd
Kate Delafield Mystery.   ISBN 0-941483-48-7   11.95

I LEFT MY HEART by Jaye Maiman. 320 pp. 1st Robin Miller
Mystery.   ISBN 0-941483-72-X   11.95

THE PRICE OF SALT by Patricia Highsmith (writing as Claire
Morgan). 288 pp. Classic lesbian novel, first issued in 1952 . . .
acknowledged by its author under her own, very famous, name.
                                            ISBN 1-56280-003-5   11.95

SIDE BY SIDE by Isabel Miller. 256 pp. From beloved author of
Patience and Sarah.   ISBN 0-941483-77-0   10.95

STAYING POWER: LONG TERM LESBIAN COUPLES by
Susan E. Johnson. 352 pp. Joys of coupledom. ISBN 0-941-483-75-4 14.95

SLICK by Camarin Grae. 304 pp. Exotic, erotic adventure.
                                            ISBN 0-941483-74-6   9.95

NINTH LIFE by Lauren Wright Douglas. 256 pp. 2nd Caitlin
Reece Mystery.   ISBN 0-941483-50-9   9.95

PLAYERS by Robbi Sommers. 192 pp. Sizzling, erotic novel.
                                            ISBN 0-941483-73-8   9.95

MURDER AT RED ROOK RANCH by Dorothy Tell. 224 pp.
1st Poppy Dillworth Mystery.   ISBN 0-941483-80-0   8.95

A ROOM FULL OF WOMEN by Elisabeth Nonas. 256 pp.
Contemporary Lesbian lives.   ISBN 0-941483-69-X   9.95

THEME FOR DIVERSE INSTRUMENTS by Jane Rule. 208 pp.
Powerful romantic lesbian stories.   ISBN 0-941483-63-0   8.95

DEATH DOWN UNDER by Claire McNab. 240 pp. 3rd Carol
Ashton Mystery.   ISBN 0-941483-39-8   11.95

MONTANA FEATHERS by Penny Hayes. 256 pp. Vivian and
Elizabeth find love in frontier Montana.   ISBN 0-941483-61-4   9.95

THERE'S SOMETHING I'VE BEEN MEANING TO TELL YOU
Ed. by Loralee MacPike. 288 pp. Gay men and lesbians coming out
to their children.   ISBN 0-941483-44-4   9.95

LIFTING BELLY by Gertrude Stein. Ed. by Rebecca Mark. 104 pp.
Erotic poetry.   ISBN 0-941483-51-7   10.95

AFTER THE FIRE by Jane Rule. 256 pp. Warm, human novel by
this incomparable author.   ISBN 0-941483-45-2   8.95

PLEASURES by Robbi Sommers. 204 pp. Unprecedented
eroticism.   ISBN 0-941483-49-5   11.95

EDGEWISE by Camarin Grae. 372 pp. Spellbinding
adventure.   ISBN 0-941483-19-3   9.95

FATAL REUNION by Claire McNab. 224 pp. 2nd Carol Ashton
Mystery.   ISBN 0-941483-40-1   11.95

IN EVERY PORT by Karin Kallmaker. 228 pp. Jessica's sexy,
adventuresome travels.   ISBN 0-941483-37-7   11.95

OF LOVE AND GLORY by Evelyn Kennedy. 192 pp. Exciting
WWII romance.   ISBN 0-941483-32-0   10.95

CLICKING STONES by Nancy Tyler Glenn. 288 pp. Love
transcending time.   ISBN 0-941483-31-2   9.95

SOUTH OF THE LINE by Catherine Ennis. 216 pp. Civil War
adventure.   ISBN 0-941483-29-0   8.95

WOMAN PLUS WOMAN by Dolores Klaich. 300 pp. Supurb
Lesbian overview.   ISBN 0-941483-28-2   9.95

THE FINER GRAIN by Denise Ohio. 216 pp. Brilliant young
college lesbian novel.   ISBN 0-941483-11-8   8.95

LESSONS IN MURDER by Claire McNab. 216 pp. 1st Carol Ashton
Mystery.   ISBN 0-941483-14-2   11.95

YELLOWTHROAT by Penny Hayes. 240 pp. Margarita, bandit,
kidnaps Julia.   ISBN 0-941483-10-X   8.95

SAPPHISTRY: THE BOOK OF LESBIAN SEXUALITY by
Pat Califia. 3d edition, revised. 208 pp.   ISBN 0-941483-24-X   12.95

CHERISHED LOVE by Evelyn Kennedy. 192 pp. Erotic Lesbian
love story.   ISBN 0-941483-08-8   11.95

THE SECRET IN THE BIRD by Camarin Grae. 312 pp. Striking,
psychological suspense novel.   ISBN 0-941483-05-3   8.95

TO THE LIGHTNING by Catherine Ennis. 208 pp. Romantic
Lesbian `Robinson Crusoe adventure.   ISBN 0-941483-06-1   8.95

DREAMS AND SWORDS by Katherine V. Forrest. 192 pp.
Romantic, erotic, imaginative stories.   ISBN 0-941483-03-7   11.95

MEMORY BOARD by Jane Rule. 336 pp. Memorable novel
about an aging Lesbian couple.   ISBN 0-941483-02-9   12.95

THE ALWAYS ANONYMOUS BEAST by Lauren Wright Douglas.
224 pp. 1st Caitlin Reece Mystery.   ISBN 0-941483-04-5   8.95

MURDER AT THE NIGHTWOOD BAR by Katherine V. Forrest.
240 pp. 2nd Kate Delafield Mystery.   ISBN 0-930044-92-4   11.95

WINGED DANCER by Camarin Grae. 228 pp. Erotic Lesbian
adventure story.   ISBN 0-930044-88-6   8.95

PAZ by Camarin Grae. 336 pp. Romantic Lesbian adventurer
with the power to change the world.   ISBN 0-930044-89-4   8.95

SOUL SNATCHER by Camarin Grae. 224 pp. A puzzle, an
adventure, a mystery — Lesbian romance.   ISBN 0-930044-90-8   8.95

These are just a few of the many Naiad Press titles — we are the oldest and
largest lesbian/feminist publishing company in the world. We also offer an
enormous selection of lesbian video products. Please request a complete
catalog. We offer personal service; we encourage and welcome direct mail
orders from individuals who have limited access to bookstores carrying our
publications.